STAR TREK
THE NEXT GENERATION

THE EXTRAORDINARY NOVEL
BASED ON THE TELEVISION EPISODE
WRITTEN BY D.C. FONTANA AND
GENE RODDENBERRY
CREATED BY GENE RODDENBERRY

STAR TREK®
THE NEXT GENERATION

ENCOUNTER AT FARPOINT

A NOVEL BY
DAVID GERROLD

PUBLISHED BY POCKET BOOKS NEW YORK

Another *Original* publication of POCKET BOOKS

POCKET BOOKS, a division of Simon & Schuster, Inc.
1230 Avenue of the Americas, New York, N.Y. 10020

This book is published by Pocket Books, a division of Simon & Schuster, Inc. under exclusive license from Paramount Pictures Corporation.

ISBN: 0-671-65241-9

First Pocket Books printing October 1987

10 9 8 7 6 5 4 3 2 1

POCKET and colophon are trademarks of Simon & Schuster, Inc.

STAR TREK is a Registered Trademark of Paramount Pictures Corporation

Printed in the U.S.A.

ENCOUNTER AT FARPOINT

Prologue

THE FIRST TIME Captain Jean-Luc Picard saw the starship *Enterprise* he was struck by the sleekness of her lines. It felt *right* to him that a ship of that size and power should also be beautiful as well. Why shouldn't starships be a demonstration of art as well as strength?

The third time Captain Jean-Luc Picard saw the starship *Enterprise,* he saw it from a different angle and he realized the designer's private joke. A quiet, almost unnoticeable smile played across his otherwise stony visage. Starships were always "she"—but this one was more feminine than most. For some reason, he liked the thought. Maybe later he would think about it some more and wonder why. Since the death of Celeste, he hadn't let himself think too much about relationships.

The seventh time Captain Jean-Luc Picard saw the *Enterprise* he was on his way to take command of her.

The tradition was that the new captain of a vessel always arrived by shuttlecraft so that he could be piped aboard. This tradition was nearly a hundred years old, and dated back to the time when the legendary Admiral James T. Kirk took command of the original *Enterprise*. (Not many people remembered that he had only boarded by shuttle because of a major transporter malfunction at the time.)

Picard wasn't a superstitious man, but this was the *Enterprise* and it wouldn't be appropriate to ignore a tradition that had begun on the first starship to bear that name.

The first time that Jean-Luc Picard walked the corridors of the new *Enterprise* he was struck by the newness of everything. It was as if this ship were somehow not yet alive, not yet *real*. That feeling would vanish quickly, he knew, but just the same he found it slightly unsettling.

He had been piped aboard by the android—

"Data?" he had asked. As if there was any doubt. The android had opalescent-gold skin and eyes so yellow they seemed to be lit from within. Its—*his*—hair was slicked straight back in an efficient, but somewhat unattractive style.

The android acknowledged its name with a nod and saluted.

Picard hesitated, then returned the salute. Formal salutes were one of those traditions that Starfleet was ambiguous about. Were they appropriate for a non-military space fleet? Were they an homage to the heritage of centuries of space travel and sea exploration before that? He appreciated the formal ritual, but he despised something of what it implied.

This moment—the first moment aboard a ship—was always uncomfortable. Picard glanced around at the honor guard standing stiffly and decided deliberately to break the stiffness. He held out his hand to

Data. "I've been looking forward to meeting you. I've been studying your record. It's extraordinary."

"Thank you, sir."

Picard noticed that the android's hand was curiously cool, too cool to be real. An odd sensation, Picard mused. Later, he would have to ask Data about its—*his*—background.

"The bridge is this way, sir."

"Thank you. May I ask you something, Commander?"

"Sir?"

"Your name? Data."

"It's self-chosen, sir. I love knowledge. Indeed, I *am* knowledge. This body is merely a container. Who I really am is the sum total of what is stored in the vessel. What better identifier for me?" Data's pleasant smile was disconcerting.

Picard nodded. It made sense.

The first time Captain Jean-Luc Picard stepped onto the bridge of the starship *Enterprise,* he was struck by how *bare* it looked. The contrast with the old *Stargazer* was startling.

There were only three officers on the bridge. It felt undermanned. They stood up to face the captain as he entered. Picard recognized Worf, the Klingon. It would have been impossible not to recognize him. The others he would meet soon enough.

He stepped down off the horseshoe at the rear of the bridge and crossed to the captain's chair. There was an air of expectancy in the room. Captain Jean-Luc Picard sat down in the chair and asked himself if he was comfortable here. The answer was yes.

"Computer?"

"Yes?"

"Can you identify me?"

"Voiceprint analysis indicates that you are Captain Jean-Luc Picard, assigned to take command of the starship *Enterprise,* NCC-1701-D, this date."

"I am now assuming command."

"So noted," said the computer.

"Activate log."

"Recording."

Picard cleared his throat. "Stardate 41150.7. Captain's log. First entry: These are the voyages of the starship *Enterprise.* Her continuing mission: to explore strange new worlds, to seek out new life and new civilizations. To boldly go where no one has gone before. Entry complete."

Picard looked around at his officers. Their faces were beaming. Abruptly, they applauded.

Picard was embarrassed, and held up a hand to stop them. "Belay that until we do something worthy of applause."

And then he retreated to his office.

He was pleased that his aquarium had already been installed. The lionfish were his only vice. They were beautiful to watch. He sat down behind his desk and installed his personal memory cartridge in the desk's reader. The ship's computer now had Picard's personal files available to it.

"I have messages for you, sir." The computer said softly.

Picard glanced at the desk screen. Most of the messages were congratulatory notes. Two of them were tagged with Starfleet Insignia. One was his formal orders. The other message was sealed orders and could not be decoded until the ship was enroute to Farpoint Station. There was also a personal message from Admiral Hidalgo.

Jean-Luc Picard was not a man for self-doubt, but . . . the starship *Enterprise* was the jewel of the fleet. There was no greater responsibility that a captain could be entrusted with. To be named captain of the *Enterprise* was an honor, an acknowledgment, and—

—and what?

There was a story, probably apocryphal, that James T. Kirk had once said that captaining the *Enterprise* was like making love in a fish bowl. You couldn't make a move without someone voicing an opinion about your technique. The statement sounded like something James T. Kirk might have said, but then again, there were more stories about James T. Kirk in circulation than *twenty* men could have lived up to—even if they had each had a Vulcan to assist them.

But . . . there was something else that disturbed Jean-Luc Picard.

This was to be the pinnacle of his career; the posting he had waited nearly twenty years to achieve. He wondered if he would be able to handle this—or if he might blow it. There had been other captains who had been entrusted with great responsibilities; good, kind, compassionate men and women who should have succeeded—and had not. Picard had studied their records, looking for that one failing that might have been common to all, looking to see if that failing was present in himself.

The only thing he had realized was the possibility of *hubris,* the pride that brings its own downfall. Each of the failures had been caused by the captain's blind faith in his or her own *rightness*. As a result, they had become rigid, inflexible. Brittle.

Picard shook his head. The thought had been troubling him lately. He reached over and tapped the message screen. Better see what Admiral Hidalgo had to say.

"You've already had my congratulations, Jean-Luc. Now it's time for a little motherly advice."

Picard smiled at that. He hadn't had any motherly or fatherly advice from *anyone* since his fortieth birthday.

Hidalgo's message continued: "I know you, Jean-Luc. You've probably been sitting there at your desk wondering if you're big enough to handle the responsibilities of the *Enterprise*. Trust me. You are." Hidalgo's broad face broke into a warm grin. Despite her age, the woman was still beautiful.

"I know you, Jean-Luc. I know that you think you worry too much. You think starship captains shouldn't worry or doubt. You think because you do that you're not a good captain. Well, now let me explain something to you, Jean-Luc. This isn't self-doubt that you're feeling. It's self-confirmation. You're going over your own decisions again to see if there's anything you've overlooked, left out, or ignored.

"That's why we selected you—or perhaps I should say that's how you selected yourself for the post. You always go the extra kilometer to be certain that you haven't made a mistake. That's why you've succeeded as a Starfleet officer. That's why we cherish your judgment. That's why you've been entrusted with the best ship in the fleet.

"And the best crew. We've given you people to be proud of. They all have extraordinary records. Use them. Trust them. Let them be the best they can. They won't let you down."

"Oh, one more thing." She added, "You're probably wondering now how I guessed that you'd be having these thoughts."

Picard grinned. Maybe it was true. Maybe Admiral Hidalgo *was* telepathic.

"It's no secret at all, Jean-Luc. *Every* captain goes through it whenever he takes command of a new vessel. I have to send this message to all my captains." She laughed. "Now let me tell you the secret of how to handle the most difficult moments of command. Always think about the very worst thing that can happen. And then don't let it happen.

"Our hearts are with you, Jean-Luc. We know you'll do well."

Picard switched off the desk screen, leaned back in his chair and laughed heartily.

Chapter One

JEAN-LUC PICARD quickly stopped counting how many times he stepped onto the bridge of the *Enterprise*. But with each new visit, he grew to love it more. The look of it, the sound of it, the smell of it. The soft murmur of the crew behind him, the occasional voices from the computers; he could sense the well-being of the entire vessel through those sounds alone.

Right now, they were satisfied sounds.

The huge Galaxy-class starship was a far cry from Picard's first command, the Starfleet exploration and research vessel *Stargazer*. She was even farther from the Constitution-class starship that had first borne the designation NCC-1701 and the name *Enterprise*.

Picard's practiced eyes glanced quickly over the bridge, noting the efficiency and smooth interaction of the duty complement. Lieutenant Natasha Yar was frowning at something on her console. The Weapons Control and Tactical Station was built into the raised horseshoe behind the captain's chair.

Tasha was one of the most physically perfect young women Picard had ever seen. She was not especially beautiful—not beautiful in the way Celeste had been beautiful, but then few women were beautiful in the way that Celeste had been beautiful. Nevertheless, Tasha was a striking woman, with piercing green eyes and a short burr of honey-blond hair.

The big Klingon lieutenant, Worf, was seated at the ship's operations station at the front of the bridge. His Klingon heritage was a source of great pride to him, and Picard had already noticed that the young officer still had some difficulty learning how to temper his natural aggression. Apparently, Worf still tended to consider himself a *soldier* first.

Picard smiled at the thought. Worf had a lot to learn. Yet there was a Starfleet adage: "Any military operation is automatically a failure." It meant that the captain of the ship had failed in his duty as a peace-keeper. There was a counter-adage as well: "The most expensive army in the world is the one that's second-best." Even in the twenty-fourth-and-a-half century, the debate about military readiness was still a troubling one.

The *Enterprise* had a larger crew complement than any of the other starships in the fleet—but the eight hundred included scientists and technicians of many types. The actual ship's operation crew was probably no larger than that aboard the old Constitution-class starships. There were also some two hundred non-crew aboard—spouses and children. That fact made Picard uncomfortable. The longer voyages of ten to fifteen years that Starfleet had decreed for the Galaxy-class ships made it inherent that starship crews bring families with them. Picard had never had to deal with such a situation before, and the idea of civilians, especially children, on board frankly bothered him.

It was something he would have liked to have

discussed with his first officer—except that he did not have a first officer in place yet. They would be taking on the last of the ship's complement at Farpoint Station, including the chief medical officer and the new Number One.

Picard had read over the record of his first officer several times, trying to get a sense of the man. Commander William T. Riker, thirty-two years old, most recently first officer of the U.S.S. *Hood* from which he would be transferring to the *Enterprise*. His service record was nearly impeccable, and he had advanced to the position of first officer relatively early in his career, which implied ambition as well as ability. If anything, Riker's record was a little *too* perfect. The man had never had to deal with the consequences of a mistake. Failure was relatively unknown to him. Picard wondered if Riker would be able to handle a disastrous circumstance—or would his self-confidence be irretrievably shattered? Despite all the simulations and tests and interviews, you never knew until it was too late whether a man was ready for responsibility or not.

Well, he would find out soon enough—when they reached Farpoint Station. Picard prided himself on his ability to manage people. He felt it came from his willingness to listen to, to empathize with, the other person's perceptions. He wanted to like this fellow Riker.

Farpoint Station—that was another puzzle. The planet was on the farthest edge of explored space. The first contact team that had beamed down to the harsh surface of the world had found the Bandi, an ancient and much diminished race, living in the one city that still remained to them. Although not spacefaring, the

Bandi appeared to have a sophisticated technology that allowed them to live in luxury while they pursued knowledge, arts and crafts. The contact team had not reported much about how the Bandi city ran, except that they had an abundance of geothermal energy. The Bandi had been otherwise evasive about their technology. Their senior official, *Groppler* Zorn, had been fascinated by the concept of Starfleet and the mighty starships that plied the vast depths of space. He had questioned the contact team extensively and finally made a startling promise. The Bandi would build a modern port and staging station on their planet if Starfleet would establish regular trade.

That had been sixteen months ago. Farpoint Station, an incredibly complex and advanced facility was now reported to be finished and waiting to serve interstellar vessels. Starfleet's best analysis teams did not know how the Bandi had managed it.

Picard's sealed orders were simple. *Find out.*

How did they do it? How could an apparently nonindustrial, pastoral society design, construct and activate the most advanced base in known space in such a short time? There was no question that Starfleet wanted to use the station, but first Starfleet wanted answers.

That could mean an extensive stay at Farpoint. The most recent surveillance team had come back knowing only as much as they had begun with. The official contact teams had produced equally fruitless results, even after months of intensive surveys. Picard would have to do better.

"Difficult," Picard murmured half aloud.

"Pardon, sir?"

Picard looked up.

His second officer, Data, was peering at him; his luminous yellow eyes were bright with curiosity.

"Starfleet's instructions. I was thinking aloud. I was thinking that will be difficult to implement. Don't you agree, Data?"

"How so, sir? Simply solve the mystery of Farpoint Station."

From Picard's left, Lieutenant Commander Deanna Troi leaned forward and smiled gently at Data. "As simple as that." The ship's counselor's voice was softly musical and lightly accented. As a half-Betazoid, she had inherited the ability to communicate telepathically with Betazoids, but her telepathic communications with other species were limited to being able to feel their projected emotions. Some she could not "feel" at all. She had learned to speak from her human father, and the gentle cadences of her speech patterns were soothing. She discerned early that people wanted to share themselves with her, and they *listened* to what she had to say. That fact had been one of the reasons she had chosen her profession. As personal advisor to the captain, she served in a liaison capacity as a translator, a buffer, a counselor between him, his crew, the ship's complement, and the life forms at their many points of call.

Picard smiled at her comment. "Yes, Data. Perhaps you see it as simply a puzzle to be solved. I see it as a problem in logistics, strategy, and diplomacy as well. The problem, Data, is that another life form built that base. How do I negotiate a friendly agreement for Starfleet to use it as a staging station and at the same time snoop around trying to find out how and why they built it? How do we do it without offending them?"

Data frowned slightly. "Query. The word 'snoop'?"

Picard blinked in surprise. "Data, how can you be programmed as a virtual encyclopedia of human information without knowing a simple word like *snoop?*"

The android paused briefly, and Picard could imagine him instantaneously scanning his prodigious memory banks. "Possibilities. A kind of human behavior I was not designed to emulate. Or a term of English vernacular I have not yet encountered. I believe it to be an archaic form. . . ." Data trailed off, frowning to himself.

"It means 'to spy . . . to sneak,'" Picard began lightly.

"Ah!" Data interrupted in delight. "To seek covertly, to go stealthily, to slink, to slither. . . ."

"Close enough—" said Picard, holding up a hand to halt the rest of Data's recitation.

Troi began to smile and she tried to suppress it.

"To glide, creep, skulk," Data continued enthusiastically. "Pussyfoot, gumshoe . . ." He trailed off, suddenly aware of the look of annoyance on the captain's face. "I understand now, sir. Thank you."

Picard opened his mouth to explain to Data that Starfleet expected him to function as something more than simply an animated thesaurus, but before he could speak, Troi gasped behind him.

She clutched at herself and nearly toppled to the floor. "Captain—"

Picard turned quickly to look at her. Troi was convulsed as if by an intense physical pain. She looked as if her mind were being *seared.* "Captain!" she gasped. "I'm sensing . . . a *powerful* presence. . . ."

"Source?" Picard snapped.

Troi blindly shook her head, unable to answer. The mental hold was loosed abruptly as a bridge alarm went off. Troi weakly slumped in her chair as the bridge complement scanned their consoles, puzzled and concerned by their readings. Data moved quickly to the console at the science position and studied the panel.

Worf frowned over his console. "Something strange on the detector circuits, sir."

His voice was drowned out by a second bridge alarm that honked loudly and demandingly. At the same time, the huge main screen at the front of the bridge flickered. The view of space ahead suddenly altered. Picard involuntarily caught his breath as a shining, sparkling grid appeared, stretching across the whole of space ahead of them. It seemed impossibly huge, but also as delicate as a spiderweb, composed of interlocking geometric shapes.

Data looked up from his console, his face only slightly perturbed—as much alarm as the android ever displayed. "The object registers as solid, Captain. Or as an incredibly powerful force field. But if we collide with either—"

Picard nodded and turned to Lieutenant Torres, the officer at the conn position beside Worf. "Go to Condition Yellow. And shut off that damned noise."

Torres' hands danced on the console, and the irritating honking alarm cut off. "Condition Yellow, sir."

"Shields and deflectors up, sir," Worf snapped. Tasha Yar had reached the comm tab on her console and tapped in a signal. She looked expectantly toward the forward turbolift.

Picard glanced quickly at the screen where the glittering grid loomed larger and clearer as the *Enterprise* approached. Then he shifted in his chair and said almost conversationally. "Full stop."

"Aye, sir," Torres responded.

On the viewscreen, the shimmering net of energy seemed impossibly close. The *Enterprise* was still nearly a light-minute distant.

"Full stop, sir—"

Suddenly, the crackling, roaring power of a lightning strike flashed across the bridge. A searing, blinding flash of light poured out of a hole in space next to Picard. Instinctively, the bridge personnel backed away from it, shielding their eyes.

The column of light shook and then resolved itself into the semblance of a human figure directly in front of Picard's command chair. There was a brief moment when the outline shimmered uncertainly—and then it stabilized into a figure.

A human figure.

Picard blinked, scarcely able to believe that what he saw before him was what appeared to be a man dressed in Elizabethan costume and ceremonial body armor. The clothing details, all in black and white and silver, were perfect—embroidery-edged neck and sleeve ruffs, tight-sleeved doublet laced up the front, paned trunk hose, patterned canions, and the netherstocks covered by knee-high cuffed boots. A short cape was slung over his left shoulder; a ceremonial sword hung at his side. The being had short hair, a pointed beard, and a moustache. The helmet was cradled in his left arm.

As soon as he realized he had coalesced into an

identifiable form, the *being* offered an elaborate court bow toward Picard. The forward turbolift doors snapped open, and the security team that Tasha had signaled began to lunge forward onto the bridge. The alien merely nodded toward them, and a miniature version of the grid spanned the turbolift door and thrust the security team back. The lift doors snapped shut on their surprised faces.

The Elizabethan turned mockingly toward Picard and extended another bow in his direction. The voice of the creature, however, was anything but courteous. "Thou art notified that thy kind hath infiltrated the galaxy too far already. Thou art directed to return to thine own solar system immediately."

Picard tilted his head almost quizzically. He considered his words carefully, decided to stall for time while he figured out who or what he was dealing with. "That's quite a directive," he said calmly. "Who are you and what gives you the right to issue such an order?"

"In words thou may understand, we call ourselves *the Q*. Or thou mayest call me that. It's all much the same thing." He fluttered his hand to indicate his elaborate costume. "I present myself to thee as a fellow ship captain that thou wilt better understand me." His voice flattened harshly. "Go back whence thou camest."

"You haven't answered my other question. What gives you the right to order that?"

Q appeared mildly annoyed. "We are greater than thee. We have achieved our superiority over millenia. *Thou* art still mud crawlers compared to us. And thou contaminatest the galaxy wherever thou goest."

Tasha Yar flicked a glance at Lieutenant Torres, who had eased around in his chair. His hand crept toward the small hand phaser on his belt. Before she could snap an order to stop him, he had drawn the phaser and started to aim it at *Q*. The alien barely bothered to look; he simply nodded at Torres. A fluttering electric blue wave enveloped the young man, cutting off the sharp scream he had started to utter. He crashed to the deck with the sound of a hard, almost brittle object as Picard leapt to his feet.

"Stand where thou art!" *Q* shouted.

Picard ignored him, fighting to control his anger as he knelt beside Torres. The man looked as if he had been *instantly* frozen. Troi moved forward to kneel opposite Picard, checking Torres for pulse and heartbeat. A white mist of evaporation rose gently from Torres' body. Troi was alarmed to feel the intense cold of his almost marble-like flesh.

"Data, call the medics!" Picard snapped.

The android reached for the left hand arm panel on the captain's chair and tabbed a control, speaking urgently to sickbay. Troi finished her brief check of Torres' body. "I don't believe it. He's frozen. Life signs are there, but slow."

Picard snatched up the phaser, prudently reversed it, and stood up to shake it under *Q*'s nose. "He would not have injured you!" He displayed the phaser. "Do you understand this—the stun setting?"

"Stun?" The alien's left eyebrow arched sardonically. *"Stunning* some life forms, Captain, can kill them. Did thine officer run a systems check on *my* form before he attempted to use that weapon? Besides, even if it would only 'stun' me, knowing humans as thou dost, wouldst *thou* be captured helpless by them? I was merely protecting myself. Now, *go back or thou shalt most certainly die!"*

"This ship isn't going anywhere until this man is taken care of."

Q studied the firm set of Picard's face, the tenseness of his stance, and snorted in amusement. "Typical, of course." He negligently flicked a damask handkerchief from a pocket in his trunk hose. "As thou wishest."

The medical team arrived at that moment in the turbolift. The barrier grid that had obstructed the security men did not appear. Dr. Asenzi, the assistant chief medical officer, shot a look at *Q*, then at Picard. The captain gestured him to Torres and he moved quickly down to the man. The medics followed, trailing emergency aids and a floating stretcher. Asenzi scanned Torres quickly and efficiently, his low voice smoothly reading out the results. Finally, he nodded to his medical team and they lifted Torres' body onto the floating stretcher and started moving him toward the forward turbolift.

"Is he still alive?" Picard asked.

"He's in cryo-sleep. We can handle it," Asenzi said; but there was something in his eyes and his tone of voice that said, "But maybe we can't." Asenzi followed the medical team into the turbolift. The doors sighed shut behind them.

Picard turned toward *Q*, who had ignored the entire interlude and turned his attention to the inspection of his elaborate costume. "This is how you demonstrate your moral superiority?"

"On the contrary. This is how I demonstrate my physical superiority." *Q* frowned abruptly, looking around the bridge as if seeing it for the first time. "I see that this costume is out of date. Thy little centuries go by so rapidly, Captain. Perhaps thou'lt better understand this." *Q* moved his hand slightly.

Again the rumble of thunder shook the bridge. The searing flash of light filled the bridge again—bright enough to be blinding even through closed eyelids. Picard could see the bones of his own hand silhouetted in the glare. When his vision returned, he could see that *Q* had changed. The beard and moustache had vanished. The Elizabethan garb had become the green officer's uniform of the 1980's U.S. Marine Corps. Three rows of medals were precisely lined up on his left breast, and the fore and aft cap sported the silver bars of a captain.

"Actually," *Q* said briskly, "the issue at stake is patriotism. You must get back to your world and put an end to the communist aggression. All it takes is a few good men."

"What? What are you talking about?"

"The evil empire, Captain—the struggle for freedom. The need to make the world safe for democracy."

Picard shook his head, as if to clear it. What was *Q* talking about? "You're still in the wrong time! That nonsense is centuries behind us!"

"But you can't deny, Captain, that you're still a dangerous, savage child-race."

"Certainly I can deny it," Picard shot back. "I agree we still were when humans wore uniforms like that *four* hundred years ago. . . ."

The Marine *Q* pushed closer to Picard, interrupting harshly. "At which time you slaughtered millions in silly arguments about how to divide the resources of your insignificant little world. And four hundred years before that, you were murdering each other in quarrels over tribal god-images. And since there have been no indications that humans will ever change—"

"But even as far back as the time of that uniform, we had begun to make progress. We had begun the work of ending hunger and disease, poverty and illiteracy. We stamped out plagues, we ended famines. We taught nations how to rebuild themselves from the devastations of war. We were children growing up. We may not have known how to do the best job, but we did the job and we learned from our mistakes. *We made progress.* Rapid progress. We are still making progress."

Q twisted his mouth sardonically. "Oh? Shall we review your so-called rapid progress?" He moved his hand again in that same little gesture. Picard didn't flinch when the thunder and lightning came again. Picard recognized it as a trick—a bit of stage magic to startle the audience, to frighten him and throw him off balance. Well, it wasn't going to work.

This time, the Marine gear changed to the stark officer's uniform of the mid-21st Century wars. Now *Q* was a Fourth World Mercenary. Harsh and ugly. Every historian's nightmare: the soldiers who could not feel, could not be afraid, and could not be stopped. The healthy, clean-shaven look was replaced by an ugly, unshaven automaton face. You pointed him at a target and gave him the order to capture it or kill it. He would not return until he did.

Q spoke and his voice sounded slow, slightly drugged, as he made his point. "Rapid progress, Captain, to where humans learned to control their military with drugs."

"And your species never made a mistake—? Never learned better—?"

A beep sounded from Worf's Ops console, and he reached out to tab a control. "Ops," he murmured. The low-voiced report brought a quick smile to his dark face. He turned toward Picard and nodded. "Sir, Dr. Asenzi reports Lieutenant Torres is going to be all right."

Q watched as a sigh of relief rippled through the bridge complement. "Concern for one's comrade. How touching."

Worf tensed as his eyes shifted from the contemptuous intruder to Picard. "A personal request, sir. Permission to clean up the bridge?" he meant *Q*.

As satisfying as it would have been to say yes, Picard shook his head. Worf started to protest, but Picard stared him down. They'd had one casualty already. Picard didn't want any more. He wouldn't risk any others until he knew what he was dealing with. Behind him, Tasha had come down the ramp from the horseshoe toward the command area.

"Lieutenant Worf is right, sir. As security chief, I can't just stand here—"

"Yes, you can, Lieutenant," Picard snapped.

Tasha wanted to protest. He could see it in her eyes. If he were still a security chief, he would want to protest as vigorously as she did. All her instincts were to fight back, to deal with this intrusion on a physical level, even if it was clear the alien was far more than he appeared to be. But he was captain now, and that was a different set of responsibilities.

Tasha lowered her eyes. "Yes, sir." The captain was right, of course. Wait and see. But Tasha didn't have to pretend she liked it.

The 21st-Century soldier form of *Q* pulled out a slender tube attached to his uniform and turned it so he could sniff something from it. Then, taking a deep breath, he murmured, "Ah, yes . . . better." The drug seemed to take hold almost immediately, and *Q* smiled sarcastically at Picard. "Later, of course, on finally reaching deep space, humans found enemies to fight there, too. And to broaden those struggles," *Q* swept a hand around to indicate Worf and Troi, "you again found allies for still more murdering. The same old story all over again."

Despite himself, despite his training, Picard found his anger rising. Who was this pompous posing popinjay? By what right did he intrude and accuse? If his manners were any indication, *Q* had no claim to moral superiority at all. Picard stepped toward the being, allowing some of his anger to show. *"No.* No. You don't know what you're talking about. You have no sense of who we are at all. The most dangerous 'same old story' is the one in front of me right now. *Self-righteous* life forms who are eager *not* to learn but to prosecute, to judge anything they don't understand or can't tolerate."

Q cocked his head to one side, eyeing Picard sharply. He laughed. "What an interesting idea. *Prosecute* and *judge?"* He took a step or two away from Picard, pondering the idea, then he turned back. "And suppose it turns out we understand you humans only too well?"

"We've no fear of what the facts about us would reveal."

"The facts about you? Oh, splendid, splendid! You are a veritable fountain of excellent ideas." He flashed a pleasant smile at Picard. "Well, now—we can proceed. Of course, there are preparations to make, Captain, but I promise you, when we next meet, we will proceed exactly as you suggest." He made the short, curt salute of the 21st-Century troops. The thunder roll and flare of blinding light carried him away.

Chapter Two

THE INCREDIBLE LIGHT faded quickly, but it was several moments more before the bridge crew fully accepted that the alien being was actually gone. They looked around with both confusion and relief.

Picard's stomach was churning. Too soon. This was happening too soon. He didn't have a first officer. He hadn't had a chance to drill his crew and get to know them. It wasn't fair. Deep space wasn't fair.

Picard touched his neck to check his pulse. It was racing. Fear? Excitement? It didn't matter. He knew what was needed now—*before anything else*—was the appearance of self-control. *Fake it till you make it,* Picard said to himself. The crew looks to the captain as the source of all well-being on the ship. So be it.

Picard glanced around the bridge calmly, "Everybody all right?" There were uneasy nods of assent. "Good." He eased himself into his command chair and looked at Data. "Any readings on the alien?"

Data shook his head. "Bridge sensors picked up nothing. Either he wasn't here or he blanked them out. As we all seem to agree on what we saw, I would assume that the alien blanked them out. Let me also suggest a third possibility: the being might not have been physically present at all. He might have been a projection or an illusion of some kind. But again, that would require some kind of blanking effect on the bridge sensors. A fourth possibility: the being may have been a telepathic projection and therefore not detectable by the bridge sensors. A fifth possibility—"

Picard held up a hand. "Thank you, Data." As always, Data not only answered the question, he practically beat it to death with alternative possibilities.

"Sir," Worf stood up before him. "I respectfully submit that our only choice is to fight."

Tasha stepped down off the horseshoe to stand next to Worf. "I agree, sir. We fight or try to escape."

Picard held up a hand to them and turned to Troi. "Did you sense anything, Commander?"

She shook her head. "Its mind is much too powerful, sir." She paused and then added, "Recommend we avoid contact."

"Interesting," Picard said. "Very interesting."

He considered their remarks, turning the situation over in his mind. There was something they could try. It might not work, but it was a fair chance they could take *Q* by surprise. He looked up at his people. "All right. From this moment, no station aboard, repeat *no station*, for any reason will make use of signals, transmission or intercom. Confine all communications to hardcopy only. My personal comm line will be reserved as the only active signals line in use. Let's see if we can take them by surprise. Lieutenant Worf, inform engineering to make ready for maximum acceleration and we'll find out what a Galaxy-class starship can do."

"Aye, sir."

Worf was already on his way to the forward turbolift as Picard turned to Data. "Records search, Data. Results of attempting battle configuration at high warp speeds."

"I beg your pardon, sir?" Data seemed honestly confused.

"You heard me. It's theoretically possible. I want to know if anyone has succeeded—or will we have to be the first?"

The android looked unhappy with the question, but he considered it, seeming to draw in on himself as he searched his internal memory banks. Then he looked at Picard impassively. "It is inadvisable at any warp speed, sir."

"Search theoretical. What are the odds?"

Data did another quick scan and lifted his shoulders in a slight shrug. "It *is* possible, sir. But there is no error margin. Therefore I cannot compute the odds."

"I see. Thank you, Data." Picard considered his idea again. It was dangerous—much more dangerous than he liked. Certainly it was much too much of a risk to ask the crew's families to accept. But . . . they were already at risk from Q—

A rock and a hard place. That was the dilemma.

Picard sighed as he examined the plan's faults and virtues one more time. It was an argument he knew he couldn't win, because he was arguing against himself. Logically, he knew what he had to do. Emotionally . . . that was another question.

Picard made a choice. He nodded to himself and stood. He raised his voice and said, *"Now hear this!"* The crew turned toward him, expectantly. He waited until there was silence on the bridge and all eyes were on him. "Using printout only, notify all decks to prepare for maximum acceleration. *Maximum,* you're entitled to know, means we'll be pushing our engines well past their safety limits. Our hope is to surprise whatever that thing is out there and try to outrun it. Our only other option would be to put our tail between our legs and return to Earth as they demand."

Lt. Worf could hurry without running. He had a stride that was near-legendary among those who had tried to keep up with him. He strode into the huge Engineering section of the *Enterprise* and paused, looking around for the officer in charge.

The great injector core dominated the center of the two-story area, driving through it from floor to ceiling. This was the heart of the *Enterprise,* as the bridge was her brain. Streams of matter were injected from the top of the core, antimatter from the bottom, to converge on the dilithium crystal, nature's wondrous gift which made warp speed possible.

Despite Klingon advances in interstellar drive technology, Worf still stood in awe of Starfleet's warp drive. It had more sustaining power and thrust than any other drive system in the combined Federation/Klingon Empire space and had been one of the key bargaining chips in the negotiations that had made them allies twenty-five years before. Klingon strategists often speculated on what would have happened had the two great powers not united. Indeed, it was a common theme of tactical games at home. Generally, the assessment was that the alliance of Federation and Empire had proven beneficial for *both*—and in some very surprising ways. But still, Worf liked to imagine what the Klingon Empire could have been had they had access to engines like these twenty-five years ago. It was a pleasant, if slightly illicit, thought.

Chief Engineer Argyle stepped in beside him quietly. "Help you, Lieutenant?"

"Captain's orders. Make ready for 'max.'"

Argyle's eyes flickered and he frowned. *"Maximum?"*

"All the way. On the signal *'engage.'*"

The chief engineer looked unhappy. He resented anyone abusing his engines. "He'd better have a damn good reason."

"We've encountered an alien force. We don't know what it is—what they are. Captain's going to see what they're made of."

"Uh uh. Captain's going to see what *we're* made of." Argyle turned toward his engineers working at their consoles. "All right. Engineering alert. Stand by. We're powering up to go to maximum warp in one jump."

Several of the engineering crew snapped around to stare at him in surprise and alarm, but he kept his face blank and noncommital. Going to maximum in one jump was hard on the ship, hard on the engines; but it could be done. They had done it in drill, they had done it in simulation. They had even *once* done it as part of the ship's shakedown.

Still . . . it wasn't considered a good idea. There was too much likelihood of phase blowout. But the crew knew their jobs, so Argyle wasn't worried about that. What was alarming was the situation that forced them to do it. "Engagement will be on captain's signal from the bridge. Blake, I'll want a maximum charge on the reserve cells."

Worf grinned wickedly and headed back to the main bridge. As the doors to Engineering hissed closed behind him, he heard the low-pitched whine of standard warp power ascending quickly to a high shriek.

Picard stood behind Data at the conn, studying the alien grid that glittered on the viewscreen. Whichever way they turned their viewer cameras, the grid barred their way—except behind them. Picard was pinning his hopes on what his ancient sporting forebears would have called an "end run."

Worf burst back onto the bridge from the forward turbolift, half running toward his operations station. "Engine Room standing by, sir."

"Thank you, Worf. Data?"

"The board is green, Captain."

The captain stepped back to his command chair and settled easily into it. "Reverse heading, 180 mark 2. Stand by." His eyes flicked over the bridge and the crew poised in readiness at their various stations. He tapped the communication tab on his left-hand panel. *"Engage!"* The entire bridge shuddered under a scream of power as the warp engines leapt to their full strength.

Picard imagined for just the briefest of instants that he could feel the acceleration as the *Enterprise* leapt forward. Of course, he could not. He'd have been smeared across the back wall if the inertial gravitational adjustors had not been in sync with the warp drive. Nonetheless, Picard *imagined* that he could feel the acceleration. Every ship captain did.

The *Enterprise* shot forward, held in control like a tightly reined horse under Data's navigation, and then—*peeled off in a stomach-churning sharp left turn!* They passed perilously close to the shimmering alien grid, but then they were beyond it and still pushing their warp envelope upward.

Still under Data's tight control, the starship angled her nose beyond the grid and raced free. Behind them, the grid wavered briefly, its glow dimming. It suddenly shrank in size, coalescing into a brightly colored spinning shape that swiftly settled into grim pursuit of the *Enterprise*.

Picard ignored the steadily rising thrum of the engines and listened to his officers as they reported. "Warp nine point two," Worf reported, grinning. He didn't approve of running from any fight—but he did understand the value of a "strategic withdrawal." Particularly a strategic withdrawal that demonstrated both strength *and* cleverness. After all, didn't the Earthers have a saying? "He who fights and runs away, lives to fight another day?" Or was it, "—lives to run another day?" Never mind.

"Heading, three-five-one, mark eleven, sir," Data reported from the conn.

"Steady on that."

Tasha spoke up from the Weapons and Tactical console behind Picard. "The hostile is giving chase, sir. Accelerating fast."

Worf stirred at his console and studied his screens. "We are now at warp nine point three, sir."

"Thank you. Let me know when we pass the red line."

"We are passing it now at warp nine point three five, sir."

"Thank you, Lieutenant. Inform engineering to maintain maximum power."

"Aye, sir."

"Continue accelerating," Picard said evenly. He looked over at Troi and half-smiled. "Counselor, at this point I'm open to guesses about what we've just met. What did you feel about it?"

She bowed her head a moment, her dark hair shadowing her face as she pondered, analyzing the sensations she had felt when *Q* was on the bridge. "It . . . it felt like something *beyond* what we'd consider a 'life form.'"

"'Beyond?' Clarify?"

"Very, *very* advanced, sir. Or . . ." Troi considered it and then nodded firmly. "Advanced or certainly very, very *different!*"

Worf turned in his chair to interrupt. "Sir, we're at warp nine point four."

"Hostile is now beginning to overtake us," Tasha chimed from behind Picard.

"Hostile's realized velocity is warp nine point six, sir," Data added calmly.

"Are you sure?" Picard regretted the words even before he finished speaking them.

Data did not bother to look back at Picard. He accepted rhetorical questions as a matter of human habit. "Of course, sir. Hostile is now within viewer range. Shall I magnify the image?"

"Do it."

The forward wall of the bridge shimmered, and the

blinking point of light that had been at the center of it suddenly jumped forward to become a spinning shape, shimmering and undefinable.

Tasha tensed, reading her console. "Hostile's velocity now at nine point *seven,* sir."

Picard leaned forward in his chair, keeping his eyes on the screen, tabbed his communications line open. "Engineering?"

Argyle's voice came back instantly. "Sir—I have to caution you—"

"Caution be damned, Engineer. We need more speed." Picard snapped off the communications line. "Go to *yellow alert.*"

Data touched a control on his console and the yellow alert alarm began to clamor loudly. Picard turned to Tasha. "Arm photon torpedoes. Stand by to fire." He was aware of Troi's alarmed glance, but he ignored it.

"Torpedoes to ready, sir."

Suddenly the ship shuddered. It was felt as a tremendous tremor throughout the bridge, and several of the crewmembers had to grab quickly for their consoles to steady themselves—and there was a sound, as if some great beast slumbering on the bottom of the blackest ocean had been troubled in its sleep, a beast better left unawakened.

Troi glanced around quickly. She felt the pulse of fear and alarm from some of them. Then the temblor eased away as suddenly as it had begun.

At the forward console, Worf was hastily punching up commands on his console. He had minored in the design and engineering of starships in his Academy days. He'd never experienced a *primal shiver* first hand, but that great shuddering groan couldn't have been anything else. It was a bad sign. Warp stress could rip the drive core apart.

"Hostile now at warp nine point eight, sir," Tasha reported evenly.

Worf quick-scanned his console. "Our velocity is holding at nine point five."

"Projection," Data said quietly. "We may be able to match the hostile's nine point eight if we push the warp engines to absolute capacity. But at extreme risk, sir."

"Now reading the hostile at warp nine point *nine.*"

Picard paused a moment, considering his options one more time. There was really not much to consider. He'd been locked into this course of action since the moment he'd ordered, "Engage." There was no changing his mind now. Finally he rose and raised his voice so it carried to all areas of the bridge. *"Now hear this.* Print-out message, urgent. All stations on all decks, prepare for emergency battle configuation maneuver."

Tasha looked to Picard in alarm. Troi looked at Tasha at the same moment, sensing her fear. The starship had been constructed so the main disk could be detached and function as an independent vehicle if necessary, although it could proceed only on impulse power. The remaining half—the stardrive section—had its own bridge, the heavy phasers and photon torpedo launchers, and the warp engines.

Original Starfleet planning designated the saucer as a sanctuary for noncombatants while the battle section was its defense. Starfleet's exploration of space had been far from uneventful, but there were only a few occasions where a captain had taken the extraordinary step of splitting his ship into two, sending the saucer section off to safety while riding the stardrive section into combat. Obviously, a captain had to consider the situation so serious that this final measure was unavoidable.

Picard gestured Worf out of his Ops chair. "You will command the main bridge, Lieutenant."

"Sir!" The young Klingon jumped to his feet in protest, his outrage overriding his normal respect for the superior officer. "I am a Klingon, sir. For me to seek escape while my captain goes into battle—"

"Noted," Picard said quickly. His voice turned cold. "But you are also a Starfleet officer, Lieutenant, and you have been given an order."

Worf hesitated, considering another protest. The years of discipline and ingrained obedience prevailed, and he nodded his head once at the captain. "Aye, sir." But his expression spoke volumes.

Picard tapped a control on his right hand panel and spoke quietly. "Captain's log, Stardate 41153.73. At this moment, I am transferring command to the battle bridge." He gestured to Data. "Make the signal."

Data touched a control lightly, and the traditional bugle call "Beat to Quarters" rang over the bridge. It repeated over and over as the duty officers swiftly moved toward the battle turbo. Replacements began to arrive almost immediately on the other two lifts, and the main bridge was fully remanned in moments.

Reluctantly, Worf moved over to the captain's command chair and contemplated it dourly before he settled down into it. "Prepare for battle configuration," he said firmly. "On the captain's command."

The thought flickered across his consciousness: *If a Klingon were in charge of this ship, we wouldn't be running.* But he was a Starfleet officer and—well, the captain might not always be right, but he was always the captain.

The turbolift fell swiftly toward the battle bridge. Picard stared unseeingly at the lift's directional lights as he considered his plan. The disengagement of the command disk at high warp speeds was a dangerous tactic, but they had to have enough of a lead on the *Q* ship (or whatever it was) so they could turn and face it while the saucer made away with the majority of the ship's company and her noncombatants.

The turbo sighed to a stop, and the doors popped open, revealing the stark and functional battle bridge. Picard led the way into the smaller station, his bridge crew quickly fanning out to their duty positions. Data activated the conn and scanned the panel while Picard quietly dictated the captain's log supplementary, explaining his strategy.

"Hostile is still closing on us, sir. Their speed is holding at warp nine point nine."

"Interesting," Picard noted. "Whoever or whatever it is, has the same warp envelope limitations as we do. Perhaps they are not so powerful as they like to pretend." Picard nodded toward Tasha. "Lieutenant, I want a full spread of photon torpedoes aimed to detonate close enough to the hostile to blind it at the moment we separate. Stand by to fire on my 'mark.'"

"Understood, sir."

Picard tabbed his communications control. "Lieutenant Worf, this is the captain."

Worf's voice replied crisply over the speaker. "Yes, sir?"

"As separation begins, we will reduce power just enough to get the saucer section out ahead and clear of us."

"Understood, sir."

"Begin countdown." Picard paused, gauging the glittering intruder on the viewscreen, then said firmly, *"Mark!"*

Tasha's fingers flew over her weapons console. "Photon torpedoes away."

The torpedoes leapt away from the *Enterprise*'s aft tubes with solid satisfying ka-chunks. Each one flashed and glittered as it sped rearward.

Tasha was a superlative weapons officer, but the timing Picard required depended largely on the assumption that the hostile was traveling at its maximum speed. If it was not—if it could still increase its faster-than-light velocity, then the torpedoes would very likely detonate behind it, losing the advantage the command disk needed to get away. Picard was counting on the limitations of the alien's technology as an ally.

"On the count," Data said. "Six, five, four, three, two, one, *separation.*"

At the rear of the saucer section, where it joined the gooseneck of the stardrive section, a crack appeared. The massive retention assemblies unlocked and pulled back into their housings. Jets of vapor hissed into vacuum as connections were pulled free.

"Captain's log. Moment of separation, Stardate 41153.75. We are now free to face the hostile."

"Good luck, sir," Worf murmured as he watched them drop away.

The great disk angled up, up and away from the cobra-shaped stardrive section. As they cleared, the locking mechanisms completed their rotation and finished up flush in their housings with a thump that was unheard in space but which was felt in the disk. Worf checked his distance and ordered the impulse engines to full power. The immediate response quickly thrust the saucer section away so the stardrive section could maneuver. The instant that the saucer section cleared the warp envelope of the *Enterprise* battle module, it appeared to vanish. The *Enterprise* and its pursuer were past it in an instant too brief to register on any instruments.

This was what Picard had been hoping for—a chance for the saucer section to lose itself in the vastness of space and make a run for Farpoint Station.

On the battle bridge, Data reported quietly, "Separation is successful, sir."

Picard found himself breathing a sigh of relief. He hadn't realized he had been holding his breath. "Grâce à Dieu. Where is the hostile?"

Data tabbed his console, and the viewscreen again showed the glint of the alien vessel at its center. The multiple flares of photon torpedo explosions were still glistening around it. Picard clenched his fist and hit his knee in triumph.

"Good timing. All stop. Reverse course."

The *Enterprise* collapsed its warp envelope and swung around to face its pursuer head on. On the huge forward viewer, Picard could see that the photon torpedoes had apparently had no effect on the *Q* ship. Despite several near-direct hits, the alien vessel remained unchanged. It drove on toward the *Enterprise* with no decrease in speed. The two ships were on a collision course.

Picard studied the viewscreen a moment longer and then said, "Hold position."

Data suppressed a surprised look and replied evenly, "Aye, sir."

"They'll be on us in minutes—" Troi began.

"I know that, Counselor."

"Will we make a fight of it, Captain?" Tasha asked. "If we can at least damage their ship—"

Picard pointed at the viewer and snorted. "Lieutenant Yar, are you recommending we fight a life form that has already demonstrated significant military superiority?" He stared at her, waiting. "If you think we have a chance of winning, I'd like to hear your advice."

Lt. Yar flushed and looked away, unable to face her captain's challenging look. He was right, of course. And she was embarrassed.

Tasha Yar knew what her worst fault was. She reacted too quickly. It was why she was a good security chief. But it was also why she often had trouble coping with situations where ship's security was compromised. She still found it difficult to allow for diplomatic and strategic considerations.

The renegade colony in which she had grown up had been lawless and murderous. Her early years had been spent surviving, and all her experience had taught her to act first and try to control a situation before analyzing it. Until she entered Starfleet Academy, she had acted on the sure knowledge that hesitation could mean death. The humanitarian principles on which Starfleet based all its decisions had at first been a shock to her. But she had listened and she had learned. . . .

Something about Starfleet's basic tenets spoke to her. Not to the person she pretended to be, or the performance she put on for the people around her, or even the person she wanted to be—it spoke to who she really was. Her secret self. The self that she had shared with no one in her life.

Starfleet's policies were based on the single assertion that *Life is sacred. Everywhere.*

Tasha had not trusted this assertion. Not at first. Her initial reaction had been skepticism and derision. The Starfleet Ethics and Moral Philosophy courses were full of those discussions. But after a while, Tasha began to realize that what they were really talking about was the same thing that she had secretly dreamed of for years.

Life as it is lived isn't necessarily the way life has to be. We can do better. We are each and every one of us, always capable of going beyond what we think are our limits. That is our history. We will do better.

Tasha realized—like the dawning of a great light—that Starfleet truly wanted the same things she did. Children did not have to die of starvation. People did not have to live in poverty. Illiteracy was not inevitable. The conditions under which she had grown up were a terrible aberration, and *not* a norm.

This was the life she had dreamed of—she could start living it today. And she had accepted that in a simple declaration: "If it is to be, let it begin with me."

And from that moment, she was never the same woman again.

But even so, there were moments—like this one—when she still responded with her old instincts. "I . . . spoke before I thought, sir. We should look for some way to distract them from going after the saucer section."

"Better, Lieutenant," Picard said, nodding approval.

"Full stop, sir," Data reported. "Holding position."

Picard looked over at Troi, who was manning the communications board. "Troi, signal the following in all languages and on all frequencies. 'We surrender.' State that we are not asking for any terms or conditions."

A ripple of consternation flowed around the battle bridge as the crew exchanged puzzled looks. *Surrender?* This from Jean-Luc Picard? Only Troi felt the calm, the confidence, the sense of *rightness* that the captain put forth. It was not a sense of failure or capitulation. Picard clearly had the conviction this was the only correct thing to do.

"Aye, sir," Troi said firmly. "All language forms and frequencies." She opened the communications channels and tied in the universal translator. *"Enterprise* to *Q.* We surrender. Repeat: we surrender. Our surrender is unconditional. We do not ask for terms."

As Troi repeated the broadcast, all eyes turned to the viewscreen where the alien hostile was seen to be rapidly bearing down on them. As it neared them, the gleaming shape began to open up, partially revealing the grid. It curved and expanded, reaching out to enclose the *Enterprise.* As it encompassed them, a cacaphony of sound tore through the ship, the scream of metal being stressed beyond its limits. The entire battle section was shaken violently, forcing the crew to grab for anything solid that they could cling to. The raging, howling sound rose to a peak, and the violence of the shaking increased. A fierce, blinding flash of light bathed the battle bridge.

Then there was silence.

Chapter Three

THE LIGHT FADED.

Picard was no longer on the battle bridge. He, Data, Troi and Tasha were seated in the prisoner's dock of an immense courtroom. The courtroom was gleaming steel and glass, stark and supremely functional. Spectators were still filing in, and a buzz of excited speculation filled the air. A cadre of soldiers was spotted around the courtroom. They were armed and appeared to be uniformly surly. The clothing, hairstyles and facial decorations of the spectators also indicated the time period was the same as the soldiers'. Picard had always enjoyed the study of history; even the unpleasant chapters had their lessons to be learned. He recognized the architecture and tone of this setting in which they had been placed as apparent prisoners.

Picard was not sure exactly how it had happened. A time warp? Not likely. Transport to a carefully prepared setting? Possible, but if so, where were the other bridge officers? Why were only he, Troi, Tasha and Data here? Had *Q* changed the battle bridge somehow? That seemed the most likely probability. *Q* had

had no difficulties changing his personal appearance when he appeared on the *Enterprise* and had ended with a characterization of this time period.

The sound of a bell drew their attention to a man at the front of the courtroom. An Asian in a long robe appeared, carrying a slim portable viewscreen. From his studies, Picard knew this would be a Mandarin-Bailiff. The man nodded to a court functionary, who once more used an ancient Oriental bell to gain attention.

"The prisoners will all stand," the Mandarin-Bailiff announced. Picard motioned to his officers to remain seated.

Data had been studying the room with great curiosity. Picard could almost feel the intensity of analyzation from the android as he catalogued the courtroom, its spectators and appurtenances. "Historically intriguing, Captain," Data commented. "Very, very accurate."

Picard nodded, his admiration held in abeyance by the feeling that this setting would be used as a weapon against them. "Mid-21st Century, the post atomic horror . . ." Picard hated the era. It had been a time of deep human crisis. Still wounded and bleeding from the terror of nuclear war, humanity had sought answers to its pain and problems through the merciless application of a new form of dictatorial government and law representing neither capitalism nor communism, but taking a few dollops from both. It had been the last of the worst Earth governments, for once it had been overthrown, humanity began to grow toward its true potential. *Q*, of course, had chosen to ignore later eras that would place humans in a better light.

The court functionary clanged the bell again. "All present, make respectful attention to honored judge!" the bailiff intoned.

The spectators, still pushing and crowding to get in, dropped into silence and stood. Some had to be prodded to their feet by the heavily armed soldiers. Picard held out his hand, palm down, to Data, Troi and Tasha, indicating they should not get up.

Troi shook her head, concerned. "Careful, sir. This is *not* an illusion or a dream."

"These courts happened in our past."

"I don't understand either, but this is real. I can *feel* that. If *Q* has created a reality here, the soldiers' guns are authentic and we could be shot if we don't obey."

"If we're on trial, *Q* won't want us shot right away," Picard pointed out.

"No, he might give us a minute," Tasha said sourly.

A soldier moved toward them, leveling his weapon at them. "Get to your feet, criminals!"

The Starfleet officers ignored him. The court functionary clanged the bell again, and the last few whispers from spectators died away. Data glanced up and nodded to indicate Picard should look in that direction. "At least we're acquainted with the judge, Captain."

Picard was not entirely surprised to see the *Q* they had met on their bridge seated at a floating judge's bench that lifted into the room. He had seized on Picard's words about prosecution and judgment with a fervor that had surprised Picard at the time. Now Picard saw *Q* had somehow created this situation in order to do exactly that—prosecute and judge. If humans would not voluntarily return to their own solar system, they would be *sentenced* to do so.

Suddenly a nearby officer fired a burst of shots at Picard's feet and advanced on him, screaming angrily. "Attention! On your feet, *attention!*" Before the captain could react, Tasha had sprung up, pivoted in and wrestled the weapon away from the man. He tried to grab her, but she easily hooked his feet from under him with one quick move of her own leg and sent him crashing to the floor on his back.

The judge's chair shot forward as Q shouted, *"You are out of order!"*

"Lieutenant!" Picard snapped.

Two other soldiers stepped forward, their weapons raised. But it was not a death sentence for Tasha. Both men fired a burst at the fallen officer. His body jumped as the automatic weapons pumped bullets into him, and the spectators cheered and applauded the performance uninhibitedly.

"The prisoners will not be harmed," Q said pleasantly. "Until they are found guilty." He passed an amused glance to Picard, who did not respond to the taunt. Q flicked his hand negligently toward the dead officer's body. "Dispose of that," he said coldly. "Now then, Captain . . ."

Picard plucked the automatic weapon from Tasha, staring her down. She hesitated, then sat back down. Satisfied, Picard took a step toward Q. "Can we assume you mean this will be a fair trial?"

"Yes, absolutely equitable."

Picard hesitated and then handed the weapon to one of the soldiers. Q floated his bench to the front of the courtroom and nodded to the bailiff. "Proceed."

The Mandarin-Bailiff consulted his portable viewscreen. "Before this gracious court now appear these prisoners to answer for the multiple and grievous savageries of their species. How plead you, criminals?"

Data moved forward slightly. "If I may, Captain. . . ." Picard gave him an abrupt nod. He had a feeling he knew in advance how this was going to go. He could see it . . . what in historical vernacular would have been called "a setup." Meanwhile, the android had turned to address *Q*. "Objection, your Honor. In the year 2036, the new United Nations declared that no Earth citizen could be made to answer for the crimes of their race or forbears."

"Objection denied!" *Q* instantly retorted. The functionary clanged the bell raucously, and the spectators cheered enthusiastically.

Picard shook his head tiredly. As he thought, they were labeled as criminals in advance, guilty until proven innocent. *Q* had already judged human past, not their present or their promise for the future, in order to brand them as unfit to venture into the galaxy with other "more advanced" races. *Q*'s next words further proved Picard's theory.

"This is a court of the twenty-first century, by which time more 'rapid progress' had caused all 'United Earth' nonsense to be abolished." He smiled triumphantly at Picard.

Tasha angrily sprang up again, poised like a fighter on the balls of her feet. "Why don't you judge what we are now?"

Picard reached out for her. "Lieutenant, no. . . ."

She shrugged him off, for once unmindful of the fact he was the captain, her superior officer, and a man she idolized. "I *must . . .*" She turned to face *Q*. ". . . because I grew up on a world that allowed things like this court. And it was people like these," gesturing toward her fellow officers, "who saved me from it. I say this so-called court should get down on its knees to what Starfleet is, what it represents—"

"Silence!" Q roared, and he waved his hand toward her. A fluttering electric blue weave enveloped her, and she instantly went rigid. Data jumped forward to catch her frozen body before it fell, then he gently lowered her to the floor.

"She is frozen in a cryonic state," Data said, "As Lieutenant Torres was."

Troi touched Tasha's cold form and uncharacteristically flared with anger. "You *barbarian!*" she shouted at Q. "You call yourselves an enlightened race, and all you know how to do is punish anyone who offends you. That woman—"

Picard gripped her arm, and she cut off her tirade. He shook his head at her. She sensed the urgent warning he was sending. Gathering her anger, she nodded back at him.

"Criminals keep silence!" the Mandarin-Bailiff chanted.

"Quite," Q agreed. "I insist upon an orderly procedure in my court." He nodded at Tasha. *"Civilized* beings know how to conduct themselves in the presence of their superiors."

"You've got a lot to learn about humans if you think you can torture us or frighten us into silence." Picard looked back to Data, who was taking pulse and heartbeat readings from Tasha. "How is she?"

"Alive—and stable, sir. Uncertain as to how long she can survive if left in this state."

The Mandarin-Bailiff turned to Picard. "You are charged, criminals. How plead you?"

Picard ignored him. Around the courtroom, the

spectators grumbled and buzzed in irritation. The spectacle they anticipated was not forthcoming, and they were angry. Q sensed their discontent and turned on the captain himself.

"How plead you? You will answer the charges, criminals."

"Just a moment ago, you promised 'the prisoners will not be harmed.' We plead nothing so long as you break your own rules."

A low, irritated mutter swept the spectators again. The criminals were supposed to act as programmed, not in this rebellious manner. What was the matter with them?

"I suggest you center your attention on this trial, Captain," Q said coldly. "It may be your only hope."

"And I suggest you are now having second thoughts about it! You're considering that if you conduct this trial fairly, *which was your promise,* you may lose."

Q laughed, a short mirthless bark. "Lose?"

"Yes," the captain said. "Keep to your agreement, and we agree to abide by your decision." He looked meaningfully at Tasha's frozen body. "Assaulting a prisoner is hardly a fair trial."

Q considered. "This *is* a merciful court," he said finally. He waved his hand downward at Tasha, and a ripple of blue light played over her. The young woman stirred, eyelids flickering. She moved stiffly at first, as though the cold had not quite left her. Then she sat up slowly, with Data assisting her.

The spectators had become disorderly again, shouting protests about this unseemly kindness on the judge's part. Some of them were standing on the benches, shaking their fists at *Q*. The judge brought his hovering bench up over their heads and hugely amplified his voice. *"Silence!"* he roared. The entire courtroom trembled under the sonic impact of his order. The quarrelsome spectators sank down into their seats again, their heads low, exchanging frightened glances.

Picard watched *Q*'s display of power impassively. He had seen bully boys throw their weight around before. And so far, *Q* had not struck him as truly superior, only more powerful. Superiority, as Picard measured it, was a matter of intelligence, consideration, and morality.

In Picard's mind, *Q* was coming up very short of mere human standards, much less the exalted superior ones he pretended to.

Q lowered his bench to face Picard again. "Continuing these proceedings, I must caution you that legal trickery is not permitted. This is a court of fact."

Picard had seen it coming, and uttered the last words at the same time as *Q*. ". . . court of fact. Yes. We humans know our past, even when we're ashamed of it. I recognize this court system as one which agreed with Shakespeare's suggestion in *Henry IV*, Part II. The first thing we do, let's kill all the lawyers."

"Which was done," *Q* pointed out equably.

Naturally, Picard thought. "Leading to the rule, guilty until proven innocent."

"Of course," *Q* agreed, still pleasantly. "Bringing the innocent to trial would be unfair." He leaned forward, smiling malevolently; and his voice boomed out once more. *"You will now answer to the charge of being a grievously savage race."*

Picard shook his head and kept his voice neutral. "We will answer specific charges. 'Grievously savage' could mean anything."

"*Obviously* it means causing harm to fellow creatures."

"Oh?" Picared asked innocently. "Such as you did when you froze a member of my bridge crew? Such as you did when you did the same to this woman? Will you be joining us in the dock?"

Q's face turned ugly. Light crackled and shimmered around him. "You fool. Are you certain you want a full disclosure of human ugliness? So be it." He flicked a hand at the Mandarin-Bailiff. "Present the charges."

The robed bailiff bowed and referred to his portable viewscreen. Then he stepped forward and presented it for Picard's inspection. "Criminal, you will read the charges against you to the court."

Picard took the proffered viewscreen and scanned a good portion of it. He looked up at *Q* and shrugged his shoulders. "I see no charges against *us*, your honor."

The judge pounded his hand on the bench top angrily. "Criminal, you are out of order!"

As if on signal, soldiers moved in on the prisoners, unslinging their automatic weapons. Two of them pressed gun barrels against Troi's and Data's heads. *Q* looked around pleasantly and his voice was conversational. "Soldiers, you will press those triggers if this criminal answers with any word other than guilty . . ." Firing actions were thumbed to full cock, and *Q* turned to Picard. "*Criminal,* how plead you?"

Picard took his time, gauging the situation. Data, of course, was rock steady, totally without fear. The android did not know what the word meant as applied to him. Troi's eyes were wide with apprehension, but that may have meant she was picking up the aggressive tension in the room. One of the soldiers shifted his weight, anxious, anticipating that Picard's delay meant opposition. Tasha stood by his side, ready as always to fight.

But here, Picard thought, *to fight is to die. And that I am not ready to do.*

"Your honor," he said slowly, "we plead guilty." The soldiers around him relaxed, the tension in the air lessened. Data studied him curiously, Tasha anxiously. *Q* leaned back in his chair, a smile of satisfaction on his face.

"Provisionally so," Picard added.

The soldiers' grips tightened on their weapons. They looked to *Q* for guidance. The alien considered the rebellious, intractable human captain. Finally, *Q* nodded.

"The court will hear the provision."

"We question whether this court is abiding by its own trial instructions. Do I have permission to have Lieutenant Commander Data repeat the record?"

"I warn you, Captain, there will be no legal trickery!" *Q* snapped.

"Does your superior race resort to those tactics?" Picard asked. "I assure you these will be your own words." The captain pressed ahead immediately before *Q* could interrupt. "Data, exactly what followed his Honor's statement that the prisoners would not be harmed?"

Data looked inward, reviewing his information banks. Then he straightened up and inclined his head toward *Q*. "The captain asked the question. . . ." His voice changed to Picard's. "Can we assume this will be a fair trial?" His voice reverted to his own pleasant tenor. "And in reply, the Judge stated. . . ." His voice shifted to emulate Q. "Yes, absolutely equitable."

Q angrily retorted, *"Immaterial* testimony, entirely immaterial!"

Picard gestured to Data to fall silent. "If your Honor pleases, there is a simple way to clear up this disagreement." Q lifted his gavel again, but Picard raised his voice forcefully. "We *can* clear up this disagreement."

Q paused, studying Picard. The captain rushed ahead. "We agree there is evidence to support the court's contention that humans have been murderous and dangerous. Therefore, I say test us. Test whether this is *presently* true of humans."

Q suddenly snapped alert, perhaps sensing danger. "I see." He studied Picard. "And you petition the court to accept you and your comrades as proof of what humanity has become."

"There should be many ways we can be tested," Picard pointed out. "We have a long mission ahead of us. . . ."

"Yes . . . yes!" Q said, an idea forming in his head. "Another brilliant suggestion, Captain. But your test hardly requires a long mission." Q laughed sardonically, seeming to savor a special bit of knowledge. "Your immediate destination offers more challenge than you can possibly imagine." He smiled even more broadly, nodding his head in satisfaction. "Yes, yes. Farpoint Station will be an excellent test."

Picard glanced at the others. Data wore a slight frown, and the women were even more concerned. Q knew exactly where they were bound—moreover, he somehow knew exactly what awaited them there. Now the mystery Starfleet had given Picard to solve took on even greater import—and danger. But there was no point in asking *Q* to enlighten them. It was all part of the game he was playing—by his rules, on his ground. The *Enterprise* and even Farpoint Station were merely the game pieces. Picard and *Q* were the opposing players. Humanity's continuing presence on the board of space was the prize.

The Mandarin-Bailiff stood as *Q* nodded in signal to him. "Stand respectfully!" he shouted. "All present, respectfully stand!" The spectators promptly stood. Picard jerked his head, and the others rose to join him.

Q maneuvered his floating bench into position in front of the prisoners and addressed the spectators. "This trial is adjourned to allow the criminals to be tested."

The Mandarin-Bailiff signaled to the functionary, who promptly rang the Oriental bell twice. The bailiff's voice resounded over the clanging. "This honorable court is adjourned!"

Picard looked around, surprised to see the soldiers shoulder their weapons and start to march out with the milling spectators. Apparently they were free. *Q* turned toward them, the sardonic smile twisting his mouth again.

"You are a clever human, Captain, but you may find you are not nearly clever enough to deal with what lies ahead for you. It may have been better to accept sentence here."

"Sentence from you? On your terms? Sorry. If we're going to be tested, we prefer it to be on even terms."

"I'm sure you would. How do you know it will be?" Laughing, *Q* waved his hand toward them.

Picard turned his head away from the fiercely blinding light. As it died away, and he blinked his eyes to clear them of the dancing dots left by the abrupt flash, he became aware of the familiar hum and murmur of computers and bridge instruments. Focusing, he realized he was back on the battle bridge, seated in his command chair. Troi, Data and Tasha were also at their correct stations, all of them blinking and rubbing their eyes, disoriented by the abrupt change. The rest of the battle bridge complement did not seem to have noticed either the stunningly bright flash or the fact that Picard and the others had reappeared at their stations.

Data turned to the Ops officer beside him at the forward console and ventured a question. "What is the present course, Conn?"

The other officer stared at him in surprise. "Exactly what the captain ordered, sir. Direct heading to Farpoint Station." The man was distinctly puzzled by the question, and even more puzzled when Data ran a quick review of his own console and turned to Picard.

"Confirm we *are* on that heading, sir."

"Of course we are," Conn said. "I told you."

Picard cleared his throat. "Any sign of the hostile?"

Conn shot him another puzzled look, clearly wondering what was going on. "Not since they cleared off at top speed ten minutes ago. No explanation, no offensive action after that chase they put us through. I don't understand what it was all about, do you, sir?"

"Never mind, Lieutenant," Picard said. "I'm sure it'll straighten itself out at Farpoint Station." He speculated that the "time" they had spent in *Q*'s court had been subjective, and perhaps had never occurred anywhere but in their own minds. He, Tasha, Troi and Data had all been under the same influence—something so strong even Troi had felt it was real. But no one on the bridge had missed them, implying they had never been gone. The only other alternative explanation was that while they were physically removed from the bridge for some time, the crew had been under an illusion they were still there and functioning normally. Whatever the answer, it was obvious that Q had even more powerful abilities than previously suspected. The alien had implied the "test" waiting for them at Farpoint might be controlled by him. But was it—or was that, too, another carefully calculated trick?

Conn idly turned to Data and asked, "Know anything about Farpoint Station? It sounds like a pretty dull place . . . hasn't even been broken in by Starfleet yet."

Picard leaned forward in his chair before Data could reply. "Actually, Conn," he said quietly, "We've heard we may find it rather exciting."

Chapter Four

THE FIRST TIME Commander William T. Riker saw
Deneb IV was on the U.S.S. *Hood*'s viewscreens. It
was a yellowish ball of a planet with shreds of cloud
layer flat against it like tatters of pressed lace. Up
close, its surface was harsh and forbidding, covered
with mountains and huge patches of desert and subject to fierce storms that swept its surface like a
scouring pad.

The single inhabited city lay attached to the gleaming sprawl of the modern spaceport which had been
dubbed Farpoint Station. Riker had seen holograms
of some of the other cities the Bandi had built and
subsequently abandoned. The older cities seemed to
have been worn down by the elements, some to mere
ridges in the land; but the one attached to Farpoint
was far more interesting, far more advanced in its
technology. Riker had not been able to determine
whether the Bandi had outgrown the cities they built
and moved on to construct newer, better ones or
whether there had been a consolidation of the Bandi
population from the older cities into the newest and
best one.

When Riker had beamed down from the *Hood,* he had noticed immediately the superiority of Farpoint Station's equipment, its appointments, and its eager personnel. It was the largest, most ambitious, and most elaborate station he had ever been on.

He was mulling these facts over while he shaved, squinting at his reflection in the mirror that dominated a wall of one of the gleaming bathrooms in his suite of rooms on the station. The man looking back at him was tall, lanky but well muscled, and in good physical shape from frequent workouts in the ship's gymnasium. Shrewd intelligence and humor shone out from behind his lively blue eyes. Riker personally felt his appearance was acceptable in polite company and left it at that.

Of course, if a number of very attractive women in several different solar systems felt there was far more to him than that, who was he to argue.

He heard a sound in the living room and scraped the last of the soap off his throat before he walked out of the bathroom. A tall, graceful Bandi woman was collecting his breakfast tray. She glanced up at him and smiled. Riker returned the grin—and then remembered he was wearing only a casually wrapped towel around his waist. He grabbed for the overlapping edges that held it together to anchor it securely.

"I didn't expect anyone to be in for that tray so soon," he said.

"An hour is surely sufficient to ingest your food."

"Yes, it usually is," Riker agreed mildly.

The woman studied the plate with its almost untouched eggs, bacon and toast. The eggs were green—possibly some aberrant factor in the chickens the

Bandi raised. "It is unhealthful to leave food waste exposed to the air," she commented.

"That's a good point," Riker agreed. "If you'll excuse me. . . ."

"You did not eat your eggs, Commander Riker. Were they unsatisfactory?"

"No, no," he said quickly, not wishing to give offense. "To be truthful, after the night I had, eggs just didn't appeal to me." Green eggs in particular, he thought. The going-away party his fellow senior officers on the *Hood* had thrown for him had been a rather boisterous affair that had gone on far into the night, and he'd consumed a generous amount of the food and libations available. His stomach quivered again at the thought.

The Bandi were apparently not aware of that sort of human digestive frailty. The woman studied the eggs critically. "I see. *Not* satisfactory. You wish something else."

"No. No food at all. Don't worry about it." He apologetically indicated his state of undress. "If you'll excuse me . . . ?" he said again and ducked back into the bathroom. When he heard the woman exit, he slipped into the spacious bedroom and changed into his standard duty uniform. The new Starfleet design (black form-fitting jumpsuit, with a cranberry inset to designate command officer) was so comfortable he almost preferred it to civilian clothes. In fact, everything about his stay at Farpoint Station had been more than comfortable, to date.

When he first saw the luxury apartment he'd been given, with its two bedrooms, two baths, large living room and dining area, he had asked for something smaller and less ostentatious. To his surprise, Zorn, the *groppler* or administrator of the station, had assured him there was nothing smaller.

Many things puzzled him about the station and its personnel. He had offhandedly remarked to the Bandi woman who seemed to attend the apartment that he preferred classic oil spacescapes to the contemporary abstract holo presentations that hung on the walls. He had gone out to sightsee for a few hours and returned to find the suite walls decorated with classic Chesley Bonestell and Robert McCall paintings. They appeared to be originals, and yet he knew the genuine originals were owned almost exclusively by museums and art galleries, most of them on the planets of Sol's system. Then there had been the plants. His mother had been an avid gardener and passed her love of green and blooming things along to him. The day before, he had noticed that an Earth-like garden in the mall was inefficiently planted. The plants that needed more sun to prosper were too much in the shade, and he had mentioned the fact in passing to the *groppler*. An hour later, he had gone by the garden again and seen that the plants had all been rotated to take best advantage of the sun. Small things—but they had been changed so *quickly*.

Riker knew Starfleet was asking questions about the Bandi and Farpoint Station, questions that needed answering. He had a hunch that the *Hood*'s rendezvous with *Enterprise,* ostensibly for the transfer of personnel, was an elaborate excuse to probe for some of those answers.

Captain Jean-Luc Picard was a man he knew only by reputation, but it was a reputation for perspicacity, clear logic, and decisive action. Riker had a hunch that the captain wouldn't mind his new first officer doing a little detective work on his own. He decided to go looking for anything that might provide Picard with insight or information about Farpoint and the Bandi.

The small, comfortable lounge off the main shopping concourse had a viewscreen that could tie into Farpoint Station's sophisticated perimeter satellite system (designed to alert the control center to the approach of any space vessel). The lounge also boasted an entrance into an attractively terraced garden that led to an Olympic-sized swimming pool, but the two young Starfleet officers in the lounge were far more interested in the viewscreen.

"Come on, come on," Ensign Hughes said impatiently, "where is she?" Mark Hughes was a likable redhead, twenty-one and fresh out of the Academy. He was enthusiastic, energetic, and still inclined to talk first and consider it afterward.

His companion was a few years older, and the extra layer of experience was evident in the way he moved and spoke. "Give it some space, Mark," he chuckled. "She's practically still on her shakedown cruise."

"Geordi, they say she's never late—not since the old burrhog took over the captain's chair."

"You wouldn't be talking about the *Enterprise*, would you, Ensign Hughes?" Riker's voice had just the slightest edge as it came from behind them.

The two young officers whipped around, startled. As soon as they realized a senior officer was addressing them, they snapped to attention. "Sir. Yes, sir," Hughes barked.

Riker smiled at the automatic and traditional response of the recent Academy graduate. "You can stand at ease, gentlemen," he said. "We're not aboard yet."

"You know we're assigned to her, sir?" Hughes was nonplussed.

"Of course." The commander extended his hand. "Riker. First officer." He sized them both up as they shook hands. Hughes was tall and thin, oddly attractive in a homely way. The black officer, Geordi LaForge, was shorter, stockier, his warm smile offsetting the strangeness of the device he wore over his eyes. Riker knew LaForge had been born blind, his optical nerve endings dead. Sympathetic surgeons had installed implants when he was a baby and given him better than twenty-twenty vision using a prosthesis called a VISOR—Visual Instrument and Sight Organ Replacement.

The VISOR was actually more than just a replacement for his eyes. It allowed him to see telescopically and microscopically, as well as view the entire spectrum of light from X-ray to infrared. LaForge had also been serving on the *Hood* as conn officer; but his duty shifts had not often coincided with Riker's, and the older man knew him primarily by reputation.

"I read the service records on all new personnel on the trip out," Riker said. "Excellent academic record at Starfleet Academy, Mr. Hughes."

"Thank you, sir."

"I noticed you were also the leading scorer on the null-G ball team."

Hughes smiled and shrugged it away. "You don't play alone. I had terrific support from my team-mates."

"And you, Mr. LaForge—Captain DeSoto thought very highly of your navigation on the *Hood*. Why did you request transfer to the *Enterprise*?"

LaForge's quick smile flashed enthusiastically. "Who wouldn't, sir? The biggest, newest, fastest starship in the fleet—"

"Commanded by the best captain in the fleet," Riker interrupted smoothly. "Right, Mr. Hughes?"

Hughes colored with embarrassment, red crawling up his neck, flaming his cheeks and hairline. Riker had heard the "old burrhog" remark. Hughes met Riker's eyes bravely, but his reply was a sheepish "Yes, sir."

LaForge had been darting surreptitious glances at the viewscreen. "She's overdue, you know, sir," he said suddenly.

"That's not like Picard—what I've heard of him, anyway." Riker frowned, concerned.

"Was there something you wanted us for, sir?" LaForge asked.

"Yes." Riker dragged his attention back to the two young officers. "I'm contacting all *Enterprise* personnel in transit here on Farpoint. Starfleet is very interested in this station, and I'm trying to put together a preliminary report to give Captain Picard. I'd like you to keep me informed on anything unusual you notice."

"Unusual, sir? Like what?"

Riker considered the question. The answer wasn't easy to define. "Anything you can't explain. Anything that seems out of the ordinary. Incidents that may seem like . . . well, almost like magic."

"But this is a modern station, sir," Hughes protested. "Magic—"

"It's an alien-built station, Ensign. We don't know much about the Bandi, and I suspect we should have found out a lot more before this."

A soft chime sounded on the station's public address system, and a pleasant female voice announced, "Commander Riker. Please come to *Groppler* Zorn's office. Commander Riker, please come to *Groppler* Zorn's office."

"Excuse me," Riker said to the others. They nodded quickly, and turned back to the viewscreen.

The administrator's office was in the old city that abutted the modern station. A slidewalk carried Riker diagonally across the widest part of the complex; and when he stepped off, he had only a pleasant five-minute walk to reach his destination. The corridors of the old city were narrow and high—rather like the Bandi, Riker reflected. They all looked to be about sixty Earth-years old, even the ones Riker knew to be younger. It might have been their grayish skin that lent them such a look of age; certainly their tall, thin frames suggested the fragility of old bones.

Zorn's assistant escorted Riker into the *groppler*'s office. Zorn was waiting behind a huge, elegant desk of unusual configuration. Its drawers seemed to fit into the highly polished wood with an almost organic grace and beauty of line. The rest of the furniture— the desk chair, the side tables, the occasional chairs, even a graceful cabinet—were of different shapes but made of the same burgundy-toned wood. A beautiful selection of Earth fruit stood in a silver bowl on the desk.

The administrator rose and extended his left hand to Riker. They had met when the initial group of personnel in transit to the *Enterprise* beamed down to Farpoint. Apparently, the fine points of shaking hands had eluded Zorn, and he had gotten the procedure confused. Mumbling apologies when Riker automatically held out his right hand, Zorn switched hands and managed to get his fingers and thumb in the right position to execute the courtesy.

"I came as soon as I could, *Groppler*," Riker said, settling into a chair opposite Zorn.

"Thank you." Zorn sat down and pushed some translucent message tabs around his desk. "Your vessel *Enterprise* is overdue."

Riker flicked a look at the wall chronometer behind Zorn. "By an hour and forty minutes."

"Ah. Yes. That was the scheduled arrival time. This is unusual, is it not? I had understood Starfleet ships had the reputation for unusual punctuality. Especially this *Enterprise* of yours."

"That's right. If nothing interferes."

"Of course." Zorn nodded and hesitated. "But what could possibly interfere with a starship?"

"You'd be surprised," Riker said quietly. "'There are more things in heaven and earth, Horatio, than are dreamt of in your philosophy.'"

"Ah. I am afraid I do not understand."

Riker studied the Bandi administrator thoughtfully. Zorn was a product of his planet-bound heritage. The Bandi had detected the initial contact team in their midst almost immediately and had subsequently shown an instantaneous grasp of starship travel and communication and the fact of the Federation's presence. Yet the concept of the *dangers* inherent in space travel seemed to elude them as completely as the ritual of handshaking.

"It doesn't matter," Riker said. "A good many things can put a starship behind schedule."

"Yes." Zorn smiled pleasantly. "But I trust we have made your waiting comfortable?"

"I would say luxurious." Riker watched as the administrator shrugged it away as if it were of no moment. "Would it seem ungrateful if I ask for some information?"

"As you wish."

"I find it interesting that in the midst of your ancient culture you've managed to build a completely modern trilurium and duraplast staging station. The energy supply to your fabrication facilities must be as abundant as I've heard."

Zorn smiled enthusiastically, his teeth flashing whitely in his gray face. "Geothermal energy is the one great blessing of this planet. I will have all the details of our energy source sent to your quarters."

"Thank you." Zorn was so unforthcoming with that information, Riker was sure whatever he provided would be next to useless. "But it still seems incredible that you've built this huge station so rapidly and so . . . so perfectly suited to our—to Starfleet's needs."

Zorn delicately scooted the bowl of fruit across the desk toward Riker. "Would you care for something, Commander? I am told these fruits are considered an Earth delicacy."

"Well, if there's an apple there. . . ." Riker glanced over the selection. He saw grapes, oranges, bananas, pears, peaches, tangerines, strawberries . . . but no apple. "I guess not," he said, disappointed.

"I am sorry, Commander."

"It doesn't matter. What I was saying was—" He

glanced past Zorn to the credenza behind the desk and stared. "Well, I'll be damned." Zorn turned his head to follow Riker's gaze. There was a second bowl of fruit there, and a gleaming red apple surmounted the pile.

"Ah. Yes. There was another selection here. Please help yourself."

Riker rose and moved around Zorn's desk to pick up and examine the almost glowing red apple. "I swear I didn't notice this." He sniffed it, and the sweet aroma that filled his nostrils instantly reminded him of the apple tree that had grown in his family's back yard when he was a boy.

"Does your failure to notice it make it unwelcome?"

Riker shook his head. "Not at all, *Groppler*."

Zorn smiled confidently. "I trust it will be the same with Farpoint Station, Commander. A few easily answered questions about it won't make Starfleet appreciate it less."

Riker eyed Zorn thoughtfully. *Too smooth an answer,* he thought. *Too glib.* He took a bite of the apple, its tangy tartness arousing his tastebuds as he chewed it. Zorn waited for a reply, and Riker took his time before he finally said, "I'm sure it won't, sir." He held up the apple and smiled. "This is delicious. Thank you." He turned toward the door and tossed a final line over his shoulder. "Good morning, *Groppler* Zorn."

Zorn boosted himself out of his chair as the door closed behind Riker. He turned around and hissed angrily at the empty room.

"You have been told not to do that. *Why* can't you understand? It will arouse their suspicions. . . ." He folded his arms firmly. ". . . and if that happens, we will have to punish you. We will, I promise you!"

Hughes had discovered the soda fountain tucked in a corner of the vast shopping area of the station. Geordi LaForge loved it. It was an exact duplication of the most traditional soda fountain he had ever seen. The marble-topped counter; the taps for soda water and syrup; the covered bins for ice cream cartons; dishes of nuts, cherries, chocolate and candy sprinkles; the high stools on the opposite side of the counter—every detail was correct.

The two young officers sat at the counter enjoying the ambiance. LaForge noticed that the ceiling fans that swished the air around were beautiful reproductions of early 20th Century wooden-bladed fans. The counterman, wearing striped shirt and white pants and a white fore-and-aft cap, handed Hughes a sundae that LaForge considered pretty plain. A thick cone of vanilla ice cream decked in a coat of fudge syrup and capped with a crown of frothy whipped cream sat in a lacy silver sundae dish.

Hughes grinned happily at LaForge. "I've been waiting for one of these. The *Hood* just doesn't have a good ice cream maker. It always tastes synthetic." He dipped into the concoction, savored it, and his eyes closed as he murmured in delight. "Oh, my. . . ."

"What?"

"It's just like the ice cream my grandma used to make on the farm. Try some?"

"Nah." LaForge tilted his head, dreaming . . . remembering. "Nobody could make what I'd really like to have." The counterman watched him, listening intently. "There was only one place—in my home town—that ever made a chocolate sundae with peanut butter fudge syrup and a mound of blue whipped cream and a cherry on top." He shook his head and sighed softly. God, those were *good*.

"What was the significance of the blue whipped cream?" Hughes asked.

LaForge grinned at him cheerfully. "Who knows? That's just how they *had* to be. Last time I had one was before I left for the Academy my first year—"

The counterman reached out and gently placed before him a chocolate sundae in a traditional tulip glass, the ice cream topped with peanut butter fudge syrup, a satisfyingly high mound of blue whipped cream, and a bright red maraschino cherry on top. LaForge studied it thoughtfully for a long moment, then he picked up the spoon and tasted a big mouthful.

Hughes watched curiously. "Is it—"

"Perfect," LaForge sighed. "Just like magic." Then, realizing what he'd said, he looked at Hughes. Hughes stared back. *Just like magic.*

"I think we ought to talk to Commander Riker," LaForge said.

"Right," Hughes said, standing.

"Hold it," LaForge said, clamping a hand on Hughes' shoulder. "After I finish this."

The mall foyer was a dazzling construction of trilurium and glass, light and airy and decorated with tastefully arranged clusters of trees, shrubs and flowers, some of them Earth plants and others of alien origin. A number of Starfleet officers passed to and from the mall area through the foyer. Most of them were visitors from the *Hood*, Riker knew, down for the opportunity to look around the station. All personnel transferring to the *Enterprise* had been given transit quarters on Farpoint Station.

As he entered the foyer, he spotted Dr. Beverly Crusher and her son, Wesley. Crusher would be the *Enterprise*'s new chief medical officer. Riker knew her career record was so outstanding she had achieved the position after only thirteen years in Starfleet. She was also one of the most beautiful women he had ever seen.

"Dr. Crusher!" he called out.

Wesley looked around and then back at his mother. "It's Commander Riker."

Dr. Crusher slowed to allow Riker to join them, but she did not smile. She was naturally reserved with strangers. Riker had only met her briefly on a few social situations aboard the *Hood* on its journey out to Farpoint. She wasn't one for small talk, and after seeing how she dealt with the lines unattached male officers had offered her, Riker had decided not to approach her in that way.

He had noticed on first meeting Beverly that her face and figure would ensure that she always looked at least ten years younger than her actual age. But her deep blue eyes reflected not only a quick intelligence but a strong, vibrant personality. If she was retiring around strangers, that was her business.

Wesley, her auburn-haired son, was small, compact and brimming with the same lively intelligence, multiplied by at least four. He was only moderately good looking, but he glowed with enthusiasm for life and had a cheerful, forthcoming personality. Riker had

had a few talks with him about starship technology on the trip out. Wesley asked thoughtful questions, and Riker had discovered the boy *listened* to the answers.

"Hello, Wesley. Enjoying your stay at Farpoint Station?"

"Yes, *sir.*"

Riker realized that Beverly had acknowledged his presence and was waiting for him to proceed. "I saw you and thought I'd join your stroll. If I may." He smiled charmingly.

Beverly seemed dubious—and uncharmed. "We were planning to do some shopping."

Riker persisted. "I've been meaning to visit the mall myself. If I'm welcome?"

"Of course." She began to move to the glass doors that let into the covered airy mall. Riker strode beside her, with Wesley trailing a little to the rear, studying the two adults.

The mall followed the same theme as the foyer— sun and air, pleasant vegetation and colorful, fragrant blossoms. It was dotted with attractive shops and brightly decorated booths which dispensed food, beverages, and merchandise of all kinds. The Bandi merchants were all attentive and almost too polite to the Starfleet personnel who were buying their wares. Beverly scanned the immediate shops and booths, weighing her interest in them and ignoring Riker.

"Mom's not really unfriendly, sir. She's just shy around men she doesn't know," Wesley said guilelessly.

Beverly snapped around to him, her cheeks flaming. "Wesley!"

"An excellent policy," Riker said. "I feel the same way about ladies I've just met." He looked at Beverly

76

with an amused smile, and she was forced to smile back.

"Doctor Crusher..." Riker began. "Although we're not officially part of the *Enterprise* yet, I thought there might be something useful we could do while we wait."

Beverly glanced at him, one eyebrow rising in a question. "Useful? How, Commander?"

"Investigating some things I've noticed here." Beverly moved away from him, toward a table in front of a shop dealing in exotic materials and fabrics. The bolts of cloth were lined up on the table, several standing on end to drape the fabric for best effect. Riker trailed after the doctor and waited while she glanced over the merchandise. "Captain Picard will be inspecting this station for Starfleet. Every scrap of information we can provide him will make his job easier."

"Mmmm." Beverly seemed more interested in the cloth. Quickly, Riker detailed the things he had personally noticed—the paintings, the mysterious appearance of the additional bowl of fruit with his requested apple. Beverly listened and appraisingly fingered a fold of tangerine-colored material.

"Don't you see how questionable these incidents are?" Riker concluded.

"I'm afraid I don't. What really happened? The Bandi came in and changed the decor in your rooms —at your request. A bowl of fruit that you hadn't noticed—"

"I'm sure it wasn't there."

"A bowl that you hadn't noticed," Beverly went on firmly, "contained a piece of fruit you wanted. I really don't believe Captain Picard will find that significant." She picked up a bolt of maroon material and flared one end of it out to look at it in the light. "This would look lovely with a gold pattern in it," she said to the waiting shopkeeper. The Bandi nodded and began to look further at the bolts of fabric he had on the table. Wesley watched the man with close interest as his mother turned to look directly at Riker. "I'm sure, Commander, there are reasons for a young first officer to want to demonstrate his efficiency, his astuteness, and his energy to his new captain."

"Now just a minute—"

"But my duty and interests lie *outside* the command structure." Beverly interrupted herself as she saw Riker staring past her at something that had caught his eye. The bolt of cloth that had been plain maroon before now had an intricate silver and gold figure worked into the background.

"Isn't it nice that he happened to have exactly what you asked for?" Riker asked, with just a light touch of sarcasm.

Beverly glanced at him, then back at the merchant, who was smiling serenely and waiting for her decision. "Thank you. I'll take the entire bolt. Send it to the *Enterprise* when it arrives, charged to Doctor Beverly Crusher."

The merchant bowed and ticked off the information on a flat credit monitor that hung at his waist. Then he gathered up the bolt of cloth and took it inside the shop to be wrapped. Beverly looked around at Riker with a bemused expression on her face. Riker held out his hand, indicating a direction they could take. She nodded and walked with him.

"You were saying, Doctor?" Riker asked.

Beverly looked at him uncomfortably. "I was saying that you were inventing work in order to curry favor and impress your new captain." Her chin came up and she met his eyes squarely. "I apologize for that, Commander Riker."

"My name's Bill."

"Yes, I know."

"That gold-patterned cloth wasn't in the pile when we first looked at it, Mother. I'm sure of it," Wesley said.

"I agree." Beverly paused and looked back at the shop where the merchant had once more appeared behind the table to present his wares. "Maybe this *is* something Jean-Luc would be interested in knowing."

"Jean-Luc? You know Captain Picard?"

Wesley interrupted proudly. "He served on the *Stargazer* with my father."

Beverly put a hand on the boy's shoulder and smiled apologetically at Riker. "Wes. Commander Riker isn't interested in family history. I couldn't say I know Captain Picard personally, Commander. We met, that's all. And it was a long time ago." She frowned thoughtfully. "That incident with the cloth *was* peculiar. Tell you what, I'll keep my eyes open and let you know anything else I see."

"I appreciate it—Beverly, isn't it?"

She nodded, concealing a smile. Most senior officers were on a first name basis on any ship, but she had no intention of letting young Bill Riker get too familiar too fast. Still, his observations on the odd incidents that had occurred appeared to have some basis in fact. What were the Bandi, and what were their intentions with this staging station? Riker was correct in asking everyone he could contact to stay alert and report anything unusual for Picard's attention.

"Sir—" They turned as Geordi LaForge hurried up to them. "The *Enterprise* is arriving, but—"

"Is this an official report, Lieutenant?" Riker interrupted crisply.

"Sorry, Commander." LaForge pulled himself up to attention and delivered the message formally. "*Sir.* Lieutenant LaForge reporting the *Enterprise* is now arriving, but without the saucer section."

Riker exchanged a quick, concerned look with Beverly. "Stardrive section only? What happened?"

"No information, sir. Captain Picard has signalled that he wants you to beam up immediately."

"Our new captain doesn't waste time," Beverly observed.

"Which makes it a good rule for me, too," Riker said wryly. "Thank you, Lieutenant. I appreciate your finding me so quickly."

"Yes, sir," LaForge said. "Sir, if I may, Ensign Hughes and I noticed something earlier that we thought worth bringing to your attention—"

Riker raised his hand. "File a report with me back aboard ship." He touched the communicator worn on the left breast of his uniform. "*Enterprise,* this is Commander Riker on Farpoint Station. Standing by to beam up."

"*Enterprise* to Riker. Energizing."

The air around Riker shimmered and danced. Slowly the glittering beams covered his image, and then faded away into thin air. Beverly had never ceased to be amazed at the transporter process, even though she was fully aware of its operating principle.

Starfleet technology was replete with wonderful achievements, but the method of disassembling the corporate atoms of an object or a living being, transporting them across vast distances of space, and then reassembling them perfectly was one of their greatest. She reached out to put her arm around Wesley's shoulders and nodded to LaForge.

"If you'll excuse us, Lieutenant—now that the *Enterprise* is here, we have to make our plans to beam aboard too."

"It's only the battle section, ma'am," LaForge said. "We don't know what they've been through . . . or where the saucer section is."

Beverly looked at him levelly, her face untroubled. "Then I'm sure Captain Picard will enlighten us. When he feels it's appropriate for us to know."

Chapter Five

No ONE EVER remembered the instant of actual transportation. One was simply in one place when it began, and another when it ended.

Riker watched as the transporter effect drained away around him. Seen from inside, the glittering sparkle created by the beam was a beautiful dance of color and shifting light.

As the beam died, he flashed an automatic look of assessment around the room. It was larger than the ones on the other ships in which he had served. Its colors were muted pastels and beige and soothingly pleasant.

The transporter chief behind the control console nodded to him, but it was the tall blonde woman in ship's operations uniform who briskly stepped forward to meet him.

"Commander Riker? Lieutenant Yar, chief of security."

Riker stepped down from the transporter pad, extending his hand. "I'm pleased—"

"Captain Picard will see you on the battle bridge,"

Tasha interrupted. "This way, please." She turned on her heel and stalked off, the doors hissing open to admit her. Riker had to hurry to catch up, even with his longer strides. There was a turbolift across the corridor; and Tasha was inside it, impatiently waiting for him when he reached her.

"With the saucer section gone, can I assume something interesting happened on your way here?" he asked.

"That's for the captain to explain, sir." She turned her head to speak quietly toward the controls. "Battle bridge."

Riker studied her frankly, but she did not seem to pay any attention to his scrutiny. "Yar," Riker said thoughtfully. "I believe your security teams have won the Fleet championships three years in a row in the seek-and-protect exercises."

"That is a fact, sir. We intend to keep it that way."

"An enviable record, Lieutenant. Tell me, were you on the battle bridge when it separated from the saucer section?"

"Yes, sir."

"Would you mind telling me what happened?"

"That's for the captain to say, sir."

Riker shook his head. Maybe they're *all* a bunch of old burrhogs on this ship, he thought ruefully.

On the battle bridge, Picard was intent on the viewscreen before him. "Do we have clearance?" he snapped to Data.

The android nodded from his position at the Ops console. "Aye, sir. Into standard parking orbit."

"Make it so."

The turbolift doors snapped open, and Tasha preceded Riker into the battle bridge. "Commander Riker, sir," Tasha announced crisply.

Riker came to a halt at attention beside Picard's chair. "Riker, W. T., reporting as ordered, sir." He expected the captain to offer his hand, but Picard merely glanced at him and then to Tasha.

"Is the viewer ready, Lieutenant?"

"All set up, sir."

Picard noticed that Riker was still at attention and he waved his hand negligently. "Please stand at ease, Commander. First, we'll bring you up to date on a little . . . 'adventure' we had on our way here. Then you and I will talk."

"This way, sir," Tasha said, instantly moving toward a viewer in the aft section of the bridge.

He doesn't waste any words either, Riker thought as he followed the security chief. She motioned him into a seat in front of the viewer and leaned in past him to key the viewer on. Riker prided himself on having a keen sense of smell, keen enough to determine the exact fragrance any woman was wearing. All he could smell on Tasha was the faint, pleasant aroma of soap and shampoo: Lieutenant Yar apparently disdained the standard little "feminine" touch and contented herself with just being clean. *Interesting,* Riker noted.

The viewer fluttered, almost whited out; then began running the bridge camera's record of the most extraordinary scene Riker had ever witnessed. The alien who called itself *Q* appeared on the bridge and ordered Picard to take his ship back to Sol system or suffer the consequences. Riker leaned in closer in order to clearly hear all the details of the confrontation over the hum of routine ship's business going on behind him.

Data turned away from the Ops console and addressed Picard. "Message from Lieutenant Worf, sir. The saucer section will arrive here in fifty-one minutes. The lieutenant sends his compliments."

"Inform the lieutenant we'll reconnect as soon as they arrive." The captain pushed out of his chair and headed for his ready room, just off the port side of the bridge. As he passed Tasha, he said, "Send the commander to me when he's finished viewing the encounter file."

"Yes, sir." Tasha glanced over to where the new first officer still hunched over the viewer.

Riker shook his head and spoke aloud to no one in particular. "He calls that 'a little adventure'?"

Picard was seated at his desk in the battle bridge ready room studying a series of matter-antimatter fuel formulas on the viewer when a buzzer sounded at the door. He flicked the viewer off and called, "Come."

The door slid open, and Riker entered. The captain waved him to a seat opposite the desk. Riker slid into it, studying the man under whom he had requested service. Jean-Luc Picard was fifty-five, balding, with a hawk-like face dominated by commanding, intelligent eyes. When he chose to display it, a charmingly rueful smile softened his normally stern expression. Of average height, he held his slim, tightly muscled body ramrod straight, giving the impression of more height. Riker had been struck by the enormous presence of the man when he first met him on the battle bridge. Here, in the smaller room, he felt Picard's personality even more strongly.

The man was born to command.

"I'm sorry you had to be brought aboard in such a willy-nilly manner, Commander," Picard said in a strong baritone. "I hadn't intended to welcome my new first officer by arriving in half a starship."

Riker smiled understandingly. "This is not exactly a run-of-the-mill happening, Captain."

"It seems we're alive only because we were placed on probation . . . a very serious kind of probation. And we're still possibly under sentence."

"Sentence of what, sir?"

"Never being allowed to fare out of our own star system again. The question is—how do we prove we're worthy? And will we know we're being tested? In any event, it appears Farpoint Station will be our testing ground—" A chime sounded, and Picard looked up. "Go."

Data's voice echoed over a comm line. "The saucer section is now entering orbit with us, sir."

"Acknowledge." He paused. "Commander Riker will conduct a manual docking. Picard out."

Riker's eyebrows went scrambling up in surprise. "Sir?"

Picard snapped a challenging look at him. "You've reported in, haven't you? You are qualified?"

"Yes, sir."

"Then I mean *now,* Commander."

Riker bounced to his feet and strode from the ready room. Picard leaned back in his chair, contemplating the young first officer's back as he left the room. *Adequate, so far,* he thought. *At least he's not afraid of a challenge.* He rose and followed Riker out to the bridge.

Riker had settled himself at the control console and was studying the main viewscreen when Picard slid into the command chair. Data sat beside Riker at the Ops console, but Riker was too busy concentrating on the upcoming maneuver to pay attention to him. The viewscreen showed the rear end of the saucer section as it loomed above and ahead of the stardrive section. Riker could see the docking link area. It looked smaller than he remembered. Disturbingly small.

"Ahead—docking speed," Riker said.

Data and Tasha, as well as Picard, studied him from their own viewpoints, evaluating the new man. His hands moved easily on the console as he made his initial adjustments. His posture indicated tension, but his voice was firm and steady.

"Confirming this is a manual linkup," Data said. "No automation."

Riker did not spare him a glance. He was concentrating on the angle and speed of approach. "As ordered," he replied.

The goosenecked battle section slowly moved ahead toward the vast disk. *Still a little low,* Riker noted. "Velocity to one-half meter per second. Adjust pitch angle to negative three degrees." His hands moved over the panel, long fingers delicately tabbing in gentle adjustments. "All stations, prepare to reconnect."

The two enormous sections were even, quite close together. The battle section continued to ease forward. "Level flight," Riker intoned. "Maintain docking speed." The trailing edge of the saucer section loomed into the viewscreen, the docking link area dead ahead and growing closer. Riker's hands moved quickly over the console now. "Thrusters to station keeping, all velocities zero. Her own inertia should do the job now."

The two sections slid together smoothly. The great locking mechanisms began to rumble forward out of their sockets. Riker hit two more tabs on the control console. "Lock up . . . *now.* Docking crew complete all reconnections." He turned in the chair to look back at Picard. "Docking board is green across, sir."

A voice floated from the ship's intersystem communications. "Docking Chief to Bridge. All reconnection systems are secure."

Picard tabbed the right hand command chair panel. "Thank you, Chief. Bridge out." He stood up and nodded to Riker. "If you'll join me, Commander, we have some things to discuss."

The two men entered the turbolift, and Picard snapped "Observation Deck" at the controls as the doors sighed shut. The lift rose swiftly from the battle bridge toward the now rejoined saucer section. Riker waited for Picard to speak; he would have felt presumptuous pushing a conversation at this point.

"Reconnection is a fairly routine maneuver, but you handled it quite well." Picard knew perfectly well it was a dangerous maneuver unless the person in command had both a sharp eye and quick responses. The Academy reconnect simulator was a horror chamber for those who couldn't get the hang of the maneuver, and those who couldn't washed out of command training. They were routed into operations or sciences where their lack in that one area would never endanger a ship.

"Thank you, sir." Riker said wryly. "I hope I show

some promise." Riker was annoyed at being damned by faint praise. He had been the highest scorer of all time on the Academy reconnect simulator and had successfully accomplished the maneuver on both the *Yorktown* and the *Hood*. Judging by the appraising look he shot at Riker, Picard probably knew it too.

"I do have a number of other tests for you," the captain said mildly as the turbolift eased to a halt. The doors opened, and he gestured the younger man around a curving corridor to their left.

"Yes, sir. I thought you might." Riker was not sarcastic or disrespectful, but his tone left the distinct impression he would not be walked on.

The observation lounge Picard stepped into was a large, slightly curving room that fit smoothly into the great arc of the saucer section. The windows allowed a panoramic view of the bulk of the disk and the vast depths of space winking with the cold light of the stars. The yellowish surface of Deneb IV glowed softly below them in reflected light from its sun. Picard crossed to a wall slot, speaking to Riker over his shoulder. "Coffee?"

"Thank you, sir. Black is fine."

Picard tabbed one of the flat controls twice, and in a moment two mugs of the steaming, aromatic brew were delivered. Picard handed a cup to Riker and motioned him to be seated in one of the comfortable chairs near an observation window.

"This is not your first starship."

As you very well know, Riker thought. "No, sir. Three years as second officer on the *Yorktown* before I moved up to first officer on the *Hood*."

"Now you've transferred again—to a larger starship. Is it that you simply crave more space or that you don't like a stable environment, Commander?"

Riker grinned and shrugged lightly. "What could be more stable than a twenty-year mission?"

Picard ignored Riker's joke. "I see in your file that Captain DeSoto thinks very highly of you. I respect his opinion. One thing interests me, however. You refused to let him beam down to Altair III."

"In my opinion, sir, conditions on Altair III were too dangerous to risk exposing the captain." Riker paused and regarded Picard steadily. "I'd do it again."

"I see. A captain's rank means nothing to you."

"Rather the reverse, sir. A captain's *life* means a great deal to me. I would be failing in my duty if I allowed my captain to negate *his* duty to his ship and crew by beaming down to a planet where his life could be at risk."

The captain's voice hardened. "Isn't it just possible, Commander Riker, that you don't get to be a starship captain without knowing if it's safe to beam down or not? Isn't it a little presumptuous for a first officer to second guess his captain's judgment?"

"Permission to speak candidly, sir?"

"Always."

Riker leaned forward intently, his elbows braced on his knees, his big hands moving in eloquent gestures as he spoke. "Having been a first officer yourself, you know that assuming responsibility for the safety of the ship must, by definition, include the safety of the captain. I have no problem with following any rules you lay down. But under no circumstances will I compromise your safety. If you have a problem with my position, sir, you can forestall my transfer and put me back on the *Hood* before she leaves."

"You don't intend to back off that position?"

"No, sir," Riker replied firmly.

Picard studied him carefully, and Riker levelly returned the stare. Riker's service envelope had indicated he was an ambitious officer, but counterbalancing the ambition was the simple fact that the man was good. Crew followed him naturally; he had an affinity for communicating with people; he worked hard; and he was bright. All his commanding officers had made special note of his extra study courses in subjects relating not only to command of a starship but engineering, communications, and several sciences. If he had been an academic, Riker could easily qualify for several doctorates.

As for his obstinacy on this point of refusing to let a captain lead an away team . . .

Picard finally nodded. "I'm glad to hear it, Commander. I would have refused your transfer to the *Enterprise* if you *had* backed down." He paused. "One further thing . . . a special favor?"

"Anything, sir."

Picard cleared his throat, covering a faint stir of embarrassment. "Help me with the children."

"Sir?" Riker asked, puzzled. What problem could a self-possessed man like this possibly have with children?

"I'm not a family man, Riker, yet Starfleet has given me a ship with children aboard. Using the same kind of strength you showed with Captain DeSoto, I'd appreciate it if you can keep me from making an ass of myself with them."

"Yes, sir."

"They make me uncomfortable," Picard went on. "But, since a captain needs to have the image of 'geniality' toward them, you're to see that's what I project."

Riker carefully hid his smile, managed a serious "Yes, sir."

Picard didn't seem to notice Riker's struggle to contain his grin. "I don't know about you, Commander, but the idea of children living aboard this ship—I don't care for it. They get into things. They make a mess. There have to be special security measures to keep them out of certain areas. And they'll *all* want to get onto the bridge."

"Of course they will. And we can give them supervised tours of it. I think children learn best through experience. It's all part of growing up."

Picard threw him a jaundiced look. "My experience has been that 'growing up' has been a catch-all phrase to excuse a lot of mischief. And mischief is the last thing I need aboard the bridge of my ship." His expression softened somewhat. "However, we'll have to deal with the children elsewhere—and still run a tight ship."

"Yes, sir. We can do that."

Picard smiled and held out his hand. "Welcome to the *Enterprise,* Commander Riker."

The two exchanged a firm handshake. For the first time, Riker felt the warmth of the man under the steely captain's facade. Picard's reputation as an old burrhog was no doubt earned—but behind that Riker was sure there was a fair and understanding man of compassion.

* * *

Riker stepped from the forward turbolift onto the *Enterprise*'s main bridge, and let out a long, slow breath of appreciation. It was spacious, even compared to the *Hood*'s main bridge; and the clean lines of its architecture could not conceal the fact that it bristled with the most advanced technology Starfleet had to offer. On his left, the main viewscreen offered a huge ceiling-to-deck picture of the arc of the planet below and the glittering sweep of the starfield beyond. The control and operations consoles with their low-slung couches were immediately in front of the viewscreen. Further back, tucked into the horseshoe-shaped curve of the section that divided the rear of the bridge from the command well was the captain's chair, flanked by chairs for the first officer and the ship's counselor, plus comfortable seats for any visiting guests or ship's officers called to the bridge. Ramps led up either side of the horseshoe to the aft bridge section where instrument and computer stations were ranked for science officers, propulsion systems engineers, emergency manual override, and environmental systems. The aft turbo fitted into the bridge next to the emergency equipment lockers; and, immediately to Riker's right, was the captain's main bridge ready room. Overhead, a dome offered another view of the stars. Riker found it breathtaking, but the minimal station keeping crew on the bridge tended their business as though it were completely routine. Riker supposed he would get used to it, too; but he hoped he would never lose the proud lift of his heart that he had felt when he stepped onto the bridge the first time.

The young Klingon lieutenant (j.g.) who sat in the command chair respectfully came to his feet as he recognized the commander's insignia. The only stranger wearing that rank had to be the new first officer. "Commander Riker?"

"Yes," Riker said, stepping forward. "You are . . . ?"

"Lieutenant Worf, sir. May I help you?"

"Where will I find Lieutenant Commander Data?"

"He is on a special assignment, sir. He's using one of our shuttlecraft to transfer a senior officer back to the *Hood.*"

"Senior officer?"

Worf corrected himself. "Beg pardon, sir. A *retired* senior officer. He's been aboard since we made reconnect, inspecting the medical layout of the ship."

Riker began to smile. "Ah. The admiral."

"Yes, sir," Worf agreed. "A remarkable man."

Data led the old man along the *Enterprise* corridor with a gentle care for his fragility. The admiral was stooped, wrinkled, his skin almost transparent with his great age. What remained of his hair was a yellowy white. "When we gonna get there?" he asked in a cracked and cranky-sounding voice.

"It's not too far, sir," Data said. "Just along here. The transporter will have you on the *Hood* in a matter of seconds."

The admiral stubbornly planted his feet and straightened up as far as he could, glaring with brilliant blue eyes at Data. "Hold it right there, boy. You can just cancel that transporter talk right now. Only reason I let 'em promote me to admiral was so's I could commandeer a shuttle when I wanted one."

"But, sir—"

"And I want one now."

"Sir, the transporter—"

The admiral shoved his face into Data's and scowled fiercely at him. "Have you got some reason to want my atoms scattered all over space?" he asked belligerently.

"No, sir." If he could get a word in edgewise, Data could reason with a rhino with a toothache and a hangover. "But at your age, sir," he said diplomatically, "I thought you should not have to put up with the time and trouble of a shuttlecraft—"

The admiral's growl told him that was the wrong tack to take. "What about my age?"

"Sorry, sir. If that subject troubles you—"

"Troubles me? What's so damned troubling about not having died? How old do you think I am?"

Finally, a statement Data could make with no fear of misinterpretation. "One hundred thirty-seven years, Admiral. According to Starfleet records."

The old man's eyes narrowed as he studied Data's calm face. "Explain how you remember that so exactly."

"I remember every fact I am exposed to, sir."

The admiral leaned closer, scowling, squinting one eye to examine Data's ears. "I don't see any points on your ears, boy, but you *sound* like a Vulcan."

"No, sir. I am an android."

The admiral snorted in disdain. "Almost as bad. Built by Vulcans?"

Data blinked his yellow eyes. He felt at a loss but was determined to remain respectful to the feisty old man. "No, sir." He paused and ventured, "I thought it was generally accepted, sir, that Vulcans are an advanced and most honorable race."

The admiral stared at him a moment, and Data

noted the transition as the severe blue eyes gentled and the scowl faded. Something else—a memory perhaps—seemed to flash across the old man's mind; and he patted Data's sleeve, nodding briefly. "They are, boy. They are." His voice went gruff again. "And also damned annoying at times."

"If you say so, sir."

The admiral drew himself together, and the testy frown settled back on his face. "Well, let's get on with it. The shuttle bay now—not that damned transporter room. You got that?"

"Yes, sir. Of course." Data put a hand under his elbow and guided him toward a turbolift. "This way, please."

Admiral Leonard McCoy (Starfleet Medical Corps, Retired) curled one side of his mouth in a half smile. He had won again. This victory had been far easier than the one he had managed in order to get on the *Hood* for the journey here to see the brand new U.S.S. *Enterprise.* He had been stuck in Bethesda Starfleet Hospital when she had been commissioned out of the Mars spacedock. Damn that foolish accident anyhow! He had broken his hip and torn knee ligaments all to hell tripping over one of his great great grandchildren's toys. And why? He had been hurrying to catch a tri-holo documentary on the building of the new ship and the history she would be carrying into space—history in which he had played a part. His daughter, Joanna, had chided him that his accident was largely due to conceit. She said he had wanted to make sure his name was mentioned!

He had raged and fumed, but no amount of carrying on had been able to get him out of the hospital any sooner. Today's medicine even made some of *his* old techniques seem like primitive witch doctoring—just as Spock frequently used to remark to get his dander up—but there was still very little that could be done to make old bones mend faster than in two days. *There's a pun in there,* he thought grimly. He had been forced to watch the commissioning ceremony on the biggest and best tri-holo set available, but it wasn't good enough for him. He wanted to *be there* with the others. He had seen the other starships that had borne the name *Enterprise,* had served on three of them, until Starfleet had promoted him to admiral and command of Starfleet Medical Corps.

He had retired ten years ago and more or less settled into a comfortable life on a small but meticulously maintained farm in a still rural area of Georgia. The news of the construction of a new *Enterprise*—NCC-1701-D—unexpectedly had given him a jolting thrill, and he knew he had to see her.

That was when "Bones" McCoy began to do something he had never before done in his life. He *politicked.* He was a retired admiral . . . an old *Enterprise* senior officer . . . and he called in ancient favors and long overdue debts with charm and perseverance, until he got himself outbound on the *Hood* with the roster of new personnel meeting the *Enterprise* at Farpoint Station. After that, it had been easy to finagle a courtesy tour of the ship, particularly the medical facilities.

McCoy liked her. This *Enterprise* was bigger than any other starship in the fleet, but size alone wouldn't have endeared her to him. He could see traces of the original ship he had first known in the trim racehorse outlines of this one. She was fast; she was efficient; she was the best of her breed; and McCoy had always loved style. Her crew was, again, the best and the brightest. He had been impressed with Jean-Luc Picard, a different style of captain, but clearly a brilliant one. McCoy felt comfortable with this new *Enterprise* in his hands.

They had finally reached the shuttle bay. McCoy grunted softly, tired with the effort of walking on his still-game leg. The android turned to him, concerned.

"Are you quite all right, sir?"

McCoy nodded briefly. "Yep. Want you to remember something."

"Of course, sir."

"This is a new ship, boy, but she's got the right name. Remember that."

"I will, sir."

"You treat her like a lady. She'll always bring you home."

Chapter Six

BEVERLY CRUSHER HAD served in some of the best starbase hospitals and on several starships, but the technology at her disposal in the *Enterprise*'s sickbay was impressive beyond her wildest imaginings. Ismail Asenzi, the young doctor who would be her assistant, had covered most of the equipment and was proudly showing her the hospital beds with which the treatment room was equipped. He seemed to know his business; but Beverly noticed that he regarded the equipment, especially the computer-controlled operations, as machinery that functioned on its own without need of human attention.

"Every bed has a full set of instruments here," he said as he directed her attention to the side of the bed.

Beverly nodded and reached out to touch a contact point at the left hand side of the bed. A tray of instruments slid out, and she looked them over as she spoke. "Yes. Sterilized and examined by the ship's computer. Do you ever examine them, Doctor?"

"But it isn't necessary, Doctor. The ship's computer signals on the med-alert screen if they show any sign of damage or deterioration."

Beverly tapped the contact point again, and the tray of instruments obediently slid back into the bed. She raised her glance to Asenzi, and her voice grew measurably colder. "I didn't ask you that, Dr. Asenzi. I asked if you personally examined them."

The younger man was embarrassed. He knew it was required that physicians and surgeons check their instruments despite the computer surveillance, but he had become used to letting the machine do it because he had never found an error. "The computers have always done it," he admitted.

"You weren't taught that dependence in medical school any more than I was." Beverly's voice softened. "It's every physician-surgeon's responsibility to be sure the instruments are in perfect order. In my sickbay, that means the doctor personally examines them."

Asenzi nodded. "You are correct. I have been remiss."

"I'm sure it won't happen again." Beverly moved away toward a glossy vertical area on a nearby wall. "The L-CARS for sickbay are up to date, of course."

On this, Asenzi could be proud of himself. The Library-Computer Access and Retrieval System for sickbay was his particular concern. A patient's life could depend on the accuracy and thoroughness of the records in the L-CARS, and Asenzi spent considerable time keeping them up to date. "Everything is in order. If you wish to check them yourself. . . ."

"Thank you." Beverly turned to the panel and spoke clearly. "Computer, show me the complete results of Captain Picard's most recent physical examination." The screen promptly glowed and began to flash up written information, followed by X-rays, dental records, full record of any medications prescribed. "Very comprehensive, Dr. Asenzi. And exceptionally complete. I am going to charge you with the continuing maintenance of these records, but if you have any questions or problems, please feel free to come to me on them. Computer, cancel." The screen went dark, and Beverly swung around to face Asenzi. "I'm very pleased with the condition of the sickbay and all its equipment, Doctor. You're doing an excellent job, and I'm sure it will continue. I'd like to arrange a staff meeting as soon as possible."

"Would this evening be suitable? After dinner perhaps?"

"Very suitable. Thank you—" She broke off in mid-sentence, staring past Asenzi as the door to sickbay hissed open.

Jean-Luc Picard stepped through and stopped, looking at the two doctors. He hesitated almost uncertainly. "Excuse me. Am I interrupting?"

Beverly collected herself and found a smile. "Not at all. We were just finishing the grand tour of sickbay."

"If you'll excuse me, Doctor, I'll arrange the meeting for you. Would 2030 do?"

"Fine. Thank you."

Asenzi jerked a little bow toward Beverly and then Picard, slid past them, and glided out the door. It hissed closed behind him. Beverly and Picard stood a little apart, an uncomfortable silence resting between them.

She looks marvelous, Picard thought—*almost as if fifteen years haven't gone by.* He had never been able to forget the way she looked the first time he had seen her—nor the last, when he had had the unhappy duty of bringing her husband's body home to her. Picard shifted his weight and cleared his throat. "I thought I should come down to see you personally, Dr. Crusher."

"Am I late in reporting, sir? I had intended to see you formally when I completed my examination of the medical facilities."

Picard did not immediately answer, and Beverly let the silence lie between them. Finally, he sighed and looked at her fully. "I want you to be aware that I protested your posting to the *Enterprise.* However, I felt I should explain my reasons to you."

"Do you feel I'm unqualified?"

"Not at all. Your service record is enviable—in fact, it's the best in the entire Fleet. I have no quarrel with your professional qualifications as chief medical officer."

Beverly's chin came up defiantly. She knew someone had tried to prevent her from taking this assignment. Until this moment, she never would have thought it was Jean-Luc Picard. "Then you must object to me personally," she said acidly. "And you're going to have to work very hard, sir, to make a personal objection valid enough to Starfleet to block my permanent assignment to this ship."

"I'm only trying to be considerate of your feelings," he said slowly. "Serving with a commanding officer who would continually remind you of such a personal tragedy as your husband's death wouldn't be easy for you—" He was being compassionate. He hoped she would understand that . . .

Beverly exploded in anger, slamming her hand down on the bed beside her. "You underestimate me, Jean-Luc Picard. If I *had* any objections to serving with you, I wouldn't have requested assignment to this ship in the first place."

Picard was stunned. "You *requested* the posting?" He had made the completely opposite assumption—*before* he had the facts. He rarely ever did that. And he had been wrong.

"I've apparently misjudged your feelings in the matter," he began.

"You certainly have," Beverly snapped.

"I'll withdraw my objection to your assignment immediately." Picard turned toward the door. "If you'll excuse me. . . ."

He was almost to the door before she stirred and called after him. "Captain." He stopped and looked around at her, and for a brief instant she wasn't sure what she would say. Then she realized what she had to tell him, for his sake. "I assure you my feelings about Jack's death have nothing to do with you or my position on this ship. I intend to do everything in my power to serve the *Enterprise* as a doctor."

Picard considered and finally nodded. "Thank you, Doctor." Their shared look was not comfortable; but the hostility had gone, evaporated in an attempt at understanding.

Beverly went to the desk in her office and slumped in the chair. She hadn't meant to lose her temper; she hadn't thought she would have to defend her choice of assignment to the *Enterprise*. Fortunately, Jean-Luc Picard was the same level-tempered, thoughtful man he had been fifteen years ago when she had met him before the *Stargazer*'s second voyage. She already had her medical degree and had been in private practice for eight years when Jack came home and announced to her that he had won the assignment as the *Stargaz-er*'s first officer. He respected Captain Picard for the accomplishments achieved on the *Stargazer's* first ten-year journey of exploration and research. It was a small ship, but it was a prestige assignment to be in her crew.

Three months later, Beverly had been notified of Jack's death during an away mission on an alien planet. It had seemed like a simple survey assignment, a reconnoiter of a populated area under cover of native dress. Nothing had indicated any jeopardy. Then, suddenly, the natives had turned on the away team and attacked them. Jack had died in the surprise assault as he covered for the rest of the team until they could beam up. His body had been left behind, and the natives had not molested it. Picard had gone down himself under cover of darkness to retrieve Jack's corpse and bring it back to the ship.

It was decided Lieutenant Jack Crusher was a hero and his body should be returned to Earth for Starfleet burial. Beverly had dutifully gone to the ceremony and behaved as a fallen hero's widow should. She remembered vividly the brisk, windy November day and the heartbreaking clarity of the deep blue sky. Starfleet had gone to the limit in providing an honor guard, the Fleet band, and a missing man formation in atmosphere craft. She remembered, too, Picard's face as he stood near her; and he seemed to her a man shaken and bereaved. Jack's subspace messages home to her had indicated that they had become good friends and had developed a marvelous working rapport in the short time they had served together.

The ceremony had been deadly long for her. She

had cried all her tears when the news had been brought to her by a Starfleet chaplain and one of Jack's friends. Now all she had left was the grief and the dull, empty pain—and, of course, Jack's child. The Starfleet honor guard had removed the starry flag from the casket and meticulously folded it in the traditional triangle. She recalled the young lieutenant who had handed it to her had studied her with awe. *Hero's widow.* She thought bitterly then that she would have traded anything to be just an Earthside doctor and Starfleet officer's wife again.

The next day, she had applied for Starfleet Medical Corps. If Jack Crusher could no longer reach for the stars, she and his child would.

Wesley Crusher plunked his suitcases down in the spacious quarters allotted to him and his mother and raced off in search of other people his own age. He had no need to look at the ship's location chart to find his way to the recreation deck. He had memorized it from the information packet sent to his mother before the transfer, and Wesley's memory was eidetic. It was too late for classes to be in session, and he thought he might find other teenagers somewhere on the recreation or holodecks.

He met the Harris twins, Adam and Craig, just outside Holodeck 4. They turned out to be his own age and between them determined they would undoubtedly be in several classes together. Adam and Craig had been aboard with their parents since the *Enterprise*'s commissioning, and Wesley envied their seniority. Still, neither of the other two were the least condescending or overbearing about it. Holodeck 4 was waiting to be programmed, and Wesley opted for a steaming rain forest with a flaming red sky. When he had shown a highly developed reading sense at an early age, his mother had gotten him copies of just about every classic adventure story that ever existed. He particularly enjoyed Edgar Rice Burroughs; and, in his mind, he had often traveled with Tarzan and John Carter of Mars.

In no time at all, the three boys were swinging on vines in a warm tropical rain, splitting the air with yodeling cries. Wesley's wet hands skidded on a vine he reached for, and he plummeted to the ground with a thump. His feet went out from under him, and he landed on his back in the mud, laughing. The two other boys swung down behind him, hooting good-natured insults which he accepted with a grin.

"This is great," Wesley said as he picked himself up and made a few futile gestures at wiping the mud off his wet clothes. "I've never seen a holodeck this big."

"You wanna change it?" Adam asked. "It'll only take a minute to program it over to something else."

"We had Mount Everest yesterday," Craig put in. "The program won't let us put in an avalanche, but there's a real good Yeti to track."

"Yeah, with the programmed random factor, sometimes we even get to catch it."

Wesley felt hunger rumbling in his stomach and glanced at his chronometer. "I can't now. I have to get back for dinner. How about after that?"

"Sure," Adam said. "We can show you the ecology deck, too. Nobody minds if we go there to look at the birds and animals."

Ecology decks were nice, but Wesley had seen those

before. Sometimes the techs let the children help feed the tame animals. But Wesley had his heart set on visiting somewhere else. "I want to see the bridge."

Craig shook his head. "Can't, Wes. Strictly off limits."

"Don't they run tours or something?"

"Not on Captain Picard's ship," Adam replied. "Our dad says ninety percent of the *crew* never get onto the bridge. They don't have any business there."

"Huh. Well . . . I'll see you guys later. Ecology deck at 2015, okay?"

Craig and Adam nodded, and Wesley splashed through the rain toward the portal that led out of the holodeck. He tapped the panel beside the door, and the door slid open to let him into the corridor. As he ran down the hall, he left a sloppy trail of mud and water behind him.

A passing crewman came across the messy deck, paused to glance at the holodeck entrance, and shook his head. "Monsoon season again," he observed wearily.

Riker stood before the huge main viewscreen watching the *Hood* slowly push out of orbit. He knew the rest of the station keeping bridge crew was busy behind him while he waited there, saying goodbye in his thoughts to the ship he had served aboard for three years. The *Hood* was a fine Fleet vessel, and Captain DeSoto had given him every opportunity to grow and learn as a first officer. He would miss them both. He heard the turbolift doors open behind him and turned to face Picard.

"Getting the feel of her, Commander Riker?"

Riker met him by the captain's chair. "I'd like to take her out of orbit and step her up to warp five to see how she runs." He nodded back toward the viewscreen. "We could race the *Hood* back toward Earth for a few parsecs." He grinned cheerfully. "If you don't mind."

"I'm afraid that will have to wait for a while," Picard said drily, "though I understand the impulse perfectly. Have you signaled the *Hood?*"

"Yes, sir. Your exact message. *Bon voyage, mon ami.*"

The captain smiled briefly but warmly. "Captain DeSoto is an old friend." He stepped toward the main viewscreen as he addressed the computer. "And what was the reply, computer?"

The big viewscreen flickered and then flared blindingly with a flash of light. It dwindled into an image of *Q*, still dressed as a judge, as his voice thundered around the bridge. "You're wasting time! Or did you think I was gone?"

Picard and Riker both jumped, startled; but Picard collected himself almost immediately. Worf, who had been seated at the conn, reacted instinctively, rolling out of the low curving chair and drawing his phaser at the same moment. In two more steps, he had placed himself protectively between Picard and the screen, pointing his phaser at the image there.

"Do you intend to blast a hole through the viewer, Lieutenant?" Picard inquired evenly.

Worf glanced at the screen and then at the captain and murmured an embarrassed apology. He slipped the phaser away and allowed Picard to wave him aside, to be dealt with later.

Picard looked up at the viewscreen again, still maintaining his level tone of voice. "If the purpose of this is to test humans, your Honor, we *must* proceed in our own way."

"You are dilatory!" *Q* roared. "You have twenty-four hours! Any further delay, and you risk summary judgment against you, Captain." The brilliant white light flashed from the screen again and then subsided to a serene view of Deneb IV.

Riker looks at Picard, shaking his head. "Summary judgment?"

"*Q* appears to have a flair for dramatics. And speaking of that . . . Mister Worf."

"I'm sorry, sir."

"You reacted fast, Lieutenant," Riker said with admiration. He appreciated the Klingon's ability to arm and defend almost instantly.

"But futilely," Picard pointed out.

"I'll learn to do better, sir."

"Of course you will. We've a long voyage ahead of us." Picard nodded to dismiss Worf, and a flicker of a smile took the sting from his previous words. Worf settled gratefully back into the conn chair.

Riker waved a hand toward the main viewer to indicate the vanished *Q*. "What do we do now, sir? If they're monitoring our every move, every word. . . ."

"We do exactly what we'd do if this *Q* never existed. If we're going to be damned, let's be damned for what we really are."

The delayed arrival of both the stardrive and saucer sections had made it impossible for Picard to make an appointment to meet *Groppler* Zorn before the next day. Riker delivered his report about the peculiar incidents witnessed on Farpoint Station, and Picard ordered him back to the bridge for his duty shift. He was seated in the command chair when the strange-looking officer he had seen earlier entered the bridge.

"Lieutenant Commander Data reporting for duty, sir."

Riker looked at him closely. The officer before him was of medium height and slim. His dark hair swept back smoothly from his forehead, and his yellow eyes were bright in his golden-toned skin. "I was told you were merely escorting Admiral McCoy to the *Hood*, Mister Data. It's been some time since she broke orbit."

"I apologize, sir. The admiral detained me on board until the *Hood* was almost out of shuttle range. He insisted he wanted to make me something called a 'mint julep,' but he couldn't locate any fresh mint." He frowned in puzzlement. "Query—what is a mint julep?"

"It's an alcoholic drink, Lieutenant," Riker said. "Of Earth origin. Associated with the southern United States—and the admiral."

"Ah." Data automatically filed the information. "But of course, I don't drink."

Riker hesitated, aware of the tension building in him. Then he said, "Your personal record is classified 'eyes only' for the Captain, Mister Data—but somehow I expected you to be an alien."

"One could say that I am. I am an android created and programmed by a race alien to your own. It is all in your point of view, isn't it, sir?"

"Mister Data—" Riker began.

"You can call me Data, sir," the android interrupted. "Everyone does. Shall I run a check of ship's systems, sir? The captain likes it done once every twelve-hour cycle."

"Fine, Mister—"

"Data."

"Right," Riker said glumly. A computer as second officer of the *Enterprise*—he hated the thought of it. Logical computers were fine as far as they went, but they only knew what was programmed into them. They could not react spontaneously in new situations. He studied Data's upright back as the android sat at the Ops console running systems checks. What was Picard thinking of?

Riker rolled over in his bunk the next morning when the computer woke him at the hour he had requested. He groaned, wearily stretched his lanky frame and sat up. He had dreamt of her again, waking often because he knew it was a dream and he wanted to be free of it. But when he fell back to sleep, *her* lovely face floated to the surface of his mind, smiling at him. He had left her behind, transferring off the *Yorktown* without actually saying goodbye, running (he admitted it) from her beauty and the feeling he had for her. He was ambitious and wanted to move ahead, both in rank and in starships; and his logic told him he would move faster and further alone. When she had called him *"imzadi,"* he felt he had to leave—and quickly. He wasn't sure of the word's exact meaning, but its general import was one of permanent commitment. He hadn't liked himself for leaving, but he had finally reconciled himself to that personal weakness. Still, he had never been able to sleep well when the memories in his rebellious mind brought back her image to smile at him.

The food slot delivered a breakfast of ham, eggs, buttered toast and a steaming cup of coffee. He was halfway through it when the computer panel glowed on the wall and intoned, "Commander Riker, please report to Captain Picard in his ready room. Acknowledge."

Riker looked longingly at the plate and the cup. "Acknowledged," he said. "Is the captain in a hurry, or is a ten-minute delay acceptable to him?"

He was able to get in another gulp of coffee and turn on his shower before the computer glowed again and spoke in its pleasant voice. "Ten minutes is acceptable, Commander." Riker's "thanks" was lost in the splatter of his hot shower.

Picard was waiting for him with the offer of another cup of coffee. Riker declined and settled into the chair opposite the captain. "It's been eleven hours, sir, since *Q*—"

"I'm well aware of the time, Commander. There hasn't been one untoward incident, but I can't forget his prediction that we'll face some critical test."

"At Farpoint."

"He mentioned it specifically." Picard leaned forward and flicked on his viewscreen. "I've been going over what we know about the Bandi, the planet, the station. Incidentally, I found your report very interesting. The Bandi's source of energy, for example."

"Yes, sir. The planet's internal heat results in abundant geothermal energy, but it's about all this world *does* offer."

"And it's your belief that this is what made it possible for them to construct this base to Starfleet standards?"

Riker nodded and referred to his own notes. "We could assume they've been trading their surplus energy for the construction materials they've used. Before you arrived, Captain DeSoto had the *Hood* do several scans and transferred the results to our records here, and the *Enterprise*'s current scans confirm many of the materials used are not found on this world." He looked up at Picard and noticed again how closely the man listened. The dark eyes never strayed; his attention never wandered. "The question is, who are they trading with? Our first contact team reported the Bandi were unsophisticated in terms of space travel—"

"Which they still are."

"Yes, sir, but I'm sure you are also aware the contact team received the assurance *they* were the first interstellar voyagers the Bandi had met. So how have the Bandi been doing that off-world trading—*if* they have been—and with whom?"

"The Ferengi immediately spring to mind."

"Deneb IV is rather far out of their territory," Riker said doubtfully.

Picard smiled briefly and shook his head. "Commander, I have watched the Ferengi operate for the past twenty-five years, and I can assure you if there is a profit to be made, the Ferengi will travel the length and width of the galaxy—*twice*—to do so."

Riker had to give Picard the point. The Ferengi were a somewhat mysterious race, not yet confronted face to face by humans, but leaving their contracts behind as calling cards in many places humans were now venturing. Their existence had been first suspected fifty-four years before in a quadrant of the galaxy Starfleet had just begun to explore. Since the Ferengi Alliance was constantly pushing its boundaries outward, as was the Federation, conflicts were inevitable.

The Ferengi Alliance, as far as was known, was a union of planets under the domination of the Ferengi. Some information had leaked out over the years through prospectors, free-traders, and other itinerants that not all the races under Ferengi rule were happy. Some planets were simply in close proximity and unable to elude their influence. Some had been subjugated by armed might and were not strong enough to break free. Others were held by political ties or economic dependence. It was the economics that were key to the Ferengi.

In many ways, the Ferengi were akin to Earth's robber barons of the Nineteenth Century. They probably would have felt flattered if accused of greed. They embraced the making of a *profit* like a lover. All their dealings involved a contract and, inevitably, a profit for them. They were known to be hard and dangerous negotiators, but were also known to carry out a contract to the finest detail. In turn, they expected the opposite party to live up to the letter of a bargain in exactly the same manner. There were some harrowing stories about the fates of those who tried to renege or cheat on a Ferengi agreement.

As a race, the Ferengi men encountered were described as small and slim humanoids with brown skin, enormously strong despite their size. They were totally bald, and their cup-like ears were set forward instead of lying close to the head. No one had ever seen a Ferengi woman, which perhaps was a comment on how little—or how much—they were regarded.

"The Ferengi *could* have contacted the Bandi without Starfleet knowing about it and made it a provision of the contract that their presence was to be kept secret," Riker agreed.

"Or," Picard said, smiling, "perhaps it's like those incidents you describe in your report as 'almost magical' attempts to please us."

"Those events *did* happen, sir. If I wasn't the observer, there was at least one other person to corroborate what the witness testified. I won't say the Bandi are adept at what could be called practical magic. I would say they *appear* to be."

Picard briskly pushed to his feet as he said, "And in time we'll discover the explanation. Meanwhile, none of it suggests anything threatening. If only *every* life form had as much desire to please. Ready to beam down? I'm looking forward to meeting this *Groppler* Zorn." He keyed the door open and waited for Riker.

"I still feel there's more to it than just pleasing us, sir." Riker stood and gestured for the captain to precede him onto the bridge.

"Like something *Q* is doing to trick us?"

As they emerged on the bridge, Riker was concentrating on Picard, and the sound of the turbolift doors didn't impress itself on him immediately. "You met *Q* face to face, sir. Could he arrange something like that?"

"Farpoint Station is a very material construction, Riker. I'm inclined to believe what we saw from *Q* was an extremely powerful illusion." Picard stopped and beckoned to someone. "I've asked our ship's counselor to join us in this meeting."

The captain stepped aside, and Riker's heart dropped.

She was as beautiful in person as he recalled her in his dreams—her cascading dark hair, her deep, black eyes, her gentle smile. Her small, perfect figure still made him feel gawky and overlarge next to her.

Picard was saying something. Riker forced his face into what he thought passed for a neutral expression.

"May I introduce our new first officer, Commander William Riker. Commander Riker, Ship's Counselor Deanna Troi."

She extended her hand to him formally. She was not at all surprised to see him. Of course, Riker realized, she would have known of his appointment in the counselor's routine review of service files on new personnel. Was that why his dreams of the night before had been so vivid? Her nearness would have enhanced his unconscious perception of her.

Betazoids had a strong telepathic ability, but Troi's was diluted by her human blood. Often she could perceive the feelings and moods of other people, even aliens. However, someone with whom she was emotionally close could receive her projected thoughts clearly.

They shook hands, and her voice whispered gently in his mind. "Do you remember what I taught you, *imzadi?* Can you still sense my thoughts?" What she said aloud was, "A pleasure, Commander."

"I, ah . . . likewise, Counselor," he stammered.

Picard eyed the two of them, intuitively aware there

was something between them. "Have the two of you met before?"

"We . . . we have, sir," Riker managed nervously.

So, Picard thought. He could guess something of the answer. No ship's captain objected to relationships between officers. Riker, however, seemed somewhat uneasy. He wanted to reassure his new first officer. "Excellent," Picard said neutrally. "I consider it important that my key officers know each other's abilities."

"We do, sir," Troi said quietly. Riker shuffled his feet.

"Shall we?" Picard gestured at the turbolift and led the way toward it.

Troi smiled serenely at Riker, and her voice touched his mind again. "I could never say goodbye, *imzadi.*"

Chapter Seven

DUST WAS BEING driven around the exposed areas of
the old city by a lashing wind when Zorn's assistant
bowed Picard, Riker and Troi into Zorn's office. The
gusts rattled the windows and forced the yellow-
brown powder through even the finest openings.

Although the wind-driven dust had always been a
part of his life, it still made Zorn irritable and edgy.
The yellow pall it cast over the city depressed him. He
had been prepared to be most gracious to his visitors
until he saw the Betazoid woman with the captain and
First Officer Riker. The information on Federation
planets and races he had been given by Starfleet had
detailed the telepathic talents of Betazoids. Was she a
trap set to catch him?

His greeting to them was formal, but somewhat
abrupt. Riker noticed both that and the fact that Zorn
made no attempt to shake hands. He flicked a look at
Picard, who did not realize it was out of the ordinary.
Zorn covered it with an offer of coffee, of juices, of
pastries, anything they would like—all of which were
politely refused.

Zorn settled behind his desk opposite his guests and

folded his long gray fingers. His back was stiff and upright, and his eyes kept straying to Troi. "Yes. How may I serve you, Captain?"

"Now that the station is completed, and you have officially offered to open it to Starfleet, I have been ordered to give it a close formal inspection before making final recommendations on acceptance."

"There would be no objections to that," Zorn said, with another nervous glance at Troi. "But I am puzzled by your bringing a Betazoid to this meeting. If her purpose here is to probe my thoughts, sir. . . ."

Troi leaned forward, smiling reassurance. "I can sense only strong emotions, *Groppler*. I am only half Betazoid. My father was a Starfleet officer."

"I have nothing to hide, of course. The entire station will be open to your inspection, Captain."

"Mine, and that of my officers," Picard said pointedly. Zorn nodded, accompanying the gesture with a nervous smile.

"Yes. Of course. And your officers."

"Good," Picard said briskly, "since we admire what we've already seen of your construction techniques. To have built this entire station in the short time you did requires tremendous engineering skill. Starfleet may be interested in your constructing starbases elsewhere."

"Captain, we are not interested in building other facilities. Especially not on other planets."

Troi listened to the conversation carefully, studying Zorn's face and body language for clues which she as a trained counselor could interpret. Her senses strained toward him and easily felt his nervousness. Then, at the edge of her mind, she became aware of something else . . . something distressing and painful.

"Perhaps Starfleet could use the materials you would sell them," Picard suggested.

"But they are quite ordinary, Captain. Available on many planets."

The feeling crept deeper into Troi's mind. Dull pain. Endless. Loneliness. Hopelessness. Dimly, she could hear Riker politely interrupt Picard. She forced her attention back to the men before her.

"If I may, Captain . . .?" On the Captain's nod, Riker turned to Zorn. "Perhaps a trade, *Groppler?* Some things you need in return for lending us architects and engineers who can demonstrate your techniques? Or Starfleet would be prepared to accommodate them, pay for their services. . . ."

"Payment is not an issue, Commander. Bandi do not wish to leave their home world. If Starfleet cannot accept that small weakness, then we will be forced, unhappily, to seek an alliance with someone like the Ferengi, or—"

Troi groaned softly, unable to contain the waves of pain and distress she felt. Picard snapped around toward her instantly. "Counselor, what is it?"

Troi gathered herself, struggling for composure, steadying her voice. "Do you want it described here, sir?"

"Yes!" Picard snapped with a look at Zorn. "No secrets here if we're all to be *friends.* Agreed, *Groppler?*"

Zorn had become increasingly tense, his laced fingers almost white under the gray skin. "We ourselves have nothing to hide."

Troi moaned again, hit by another wave of emotion. *"Pain* . . . pain, loneliness . . . terrible loneliness, despair. . . ." She shook her head. "I'm not sensing the *groppler*, sir. Or any of his people. I'm sure of it . . . but it's something very close to us here."

"Zorn, the source of this. Do you have any idea?" Picard demanded.

The *groppler* shot to his feet. "No! No, absolutely not. And I find nothing helpful or productive in any of this!"

Picard rose to face him. "That's it? No other comment?"

"What do you expect of us? We built Farpoint Station exactly as you would wish to have it. A base designed to your needs, luxurious even by human standards—everything you could dream of—we did all this to please you! What more can you want from us?"

"Answers," Picard said coldly. "You've evaded even our simplest questions about it. We'll adjourn for now while we all consider our positions." He gestured Troi and Riker to their feet, and they followed him toward the door.

"Captain. The Ferengi would be *very* interested in a base like this."

Picard glanced back and seared the administrator with a scathing look. "Fine. I hope they find you as tasty as they did their past associates."

Picard didn't slam the door, but he didn't need to. He had made his point. The Ferengi were not to be trusted—even if they did not literally consume their associates. (And perhaps they *did*.) The alternatives were a mutual cooperation pact with Starfleet—or maintaining the station alone, hoping trade and passenger vessels would venture out to this as yet little-mapped sector of the galaxy.

Zorn slumped against his desk, anguished. So much

of the Bandi hope was in this station. They were a diminishing race, able to exist in any comfortable surroundings they desired, but bereft of hope of survival as a race until the Starfleet contact team had beamed down. They had been astonished at the insatiable Bandi curiosity about Starfleet and human spacefaring. The Prime Directive had been carefully explained to them, and they understood it; but Zorn had been adamant in his insistence that interference in the Bandi civilization would *save* it. Starfleet had to agree that Farpoint would be one of their staging stations. They *had* to.

Picard angrily strode away from Zorn's office with Riker and Troi hurrying after him. The Captain abruptly stopped after the first heat of the exchange had worn off him, and he turned to Troi. "Zorn's evading too many questions. Did you feel anything specific from him?"

"Nervous tension . . . frustration. Not anger. I think he was feigning that, trying to force your hand. And something else."

"Yes?"

"He was very agitated when I felt that deep loneliness and pain from somewhere nearby." Troi looked directly at the captain, troubled. "I believe he was lying about knowing its source."

Picard looked up as the chime at his ready room door rang. "Come," he called, turning off the viewscreen that had once again displayed a review of everything known about the Bandi and Deneb IV. Riker stepped in, and Picard gestured to a chair. "Riker. Sit down."

"You wanted to see me, sir?"

"Yes. As I indicated to Zorn in our meeting, I want a full inspection of Farpoint Station. A *full* inspection. You'll lead the away team."

"Full inspection. Top to bottom, sir? Examine the rivets, seams and girders?"

"You understand me completely. I want the cobwebs counted—if you find any."

"Yes, sir." Riker flashed his quick, charming grin. "We'll even keep a count on any flies in the webs."

"Who knows? It might very well be significant."

Riker hitched his chair closer to the desk and leaned toward Picard thoughtfully. "Do you think Zorn was serious about offering the station to the Ferengi? Economically, it might make sense. Maybe the Ferengi made a better offer than Starfleet for the station after it was built. It would be advantageous for them to have a base in this quadrant."

Picard shook his head. "Starfleet didn't offer the Bandi anything in the first place. They built Farpoint because *they* wanted to. On the other hand, they may be hoping to *get* an elevated monetary offer from Starfleet by throwing out the threat."

"If they really mean to turn the station over to the Ferengi Alliance, it could create a problem for Starfleet in this sector. As you said, this quadrant is far out of their territory. That's not reassuring if Zorn wasn't bluffing."

There was silence between them as they considered the implications of a genuine Ferengi involvement in the area. There were already spearheads of their trade contracts lancing into territory the Federation considered a part of its own. Diplomatic treaties usually followed close behind, and the Federation had found it would look up and discover an entire star system edged into the Ferengi Alliance. Any planets so lost had not been able to return to the Federation.

"I suggest you take Data with your away team, Commander. His analytical abilities—"

"—are those of a computer. We'll be taking tricorders, sir. The information we send back can certainly be adequately analyzed by the ship's computer."

"I see." Picard studied Riker with a new consideration. He hadn't thought the man would object to working with one of the most remarkable officers in Starfleet. Of course, if Riker didn't perceive Data as an *officer,* but only as a machine, he could not be expected to appreciate the android's qualities. "You must already know Data's personal medical-technical records are 'eyes only' to me." Riker nodded. "However, his service record is open to any senior officer. I suggest you take some time to study it."

"Yes, sir," Riker said stiffly.

"I also suggest you take the time to get to know Data himself."

"As a *person,* sir?"

Picard ignored the barely hidden sarcasm. "As a fellow *officer,* Commander Riker. I take it you have no problem accepting Klingons or Vulcans or any other alien in Starfleet in that capacity?"

"No, sir."

"You may come to find Data is easier to accept than any of them when you discover how he regards humans. To the others, *we* are aliens. Data has a different view. You would profit by exploring it."

"Yes, sir. May I be dismissed?" Riker glanced away, some color creeping into his cheeks. He was genuinely embarrassed by the quiet dressing down. "To pursue the subject?" he added.

Picard nodded curtly and turned back to his viewer. Riker stood and quickly left. Picard glanced up again as the door slid closed behind him. If he was any judge of character, Picard was positive young Commander Riker would benefit from the study.

Riker spent an instructional half hour with the android's service record. There were an enormous number of subjects in which Data was qualified as an expert. He had two degrees conferred by Starfleet. Data had been given Starfleet promotions on a regular basis and had served (with commendations from the captains) on three vessels before coming to the *Enterprise* as its second officer. If it had been the file on anyone else in the fleet, Riker would have regarded it as the record of a successful and extremely competent officer. The fact that he knew Data was an android still colored his judgment about him. Obviously, Picard saw more in him—*it*—than the mere printed facts of the record could convey. He was going to have to face the man—machine—and personally explore what he—or perhaps *it*—was all about.

Riker asked for a location on Data and was informed by the computer that the android was on Holodeck Two. He took a turbolift and stepped out on the deck as a dark-haired ensign in the uniform of operations and services walked past, and Riker called out to her.

"Excuse me, Ensign. . . ."

The young officer turned and immediately came to attention when she saw the three small gold disks of his rank. "Sir?"

"Can you help me locate Lieutenant Commander Data? I was told he's somewhere on this deck."

"Oh, yes sir. This way, please." She held out a hand, directing him toward a black surface of the corridor wall, which Riker knew was a computer interface. "You must be new to these Galaxy-class starships, sir."

"A little," Riker admitted.

The Ensign placed her hand on the black surface. *"Tell me* the location of Lieutenant Commander Data."

At the touch of her hand and the key words, "Tell me," the black surface glowed and displayed a light pattern that formed the words "Area 4-J." The computer's mellow voice intoned, "Lieutenant Commander Data . . . now located in Holodeck area 4-J." An overlay of the holodeck appeared with a glowing light path imposed on it which indicated the way from where they stood to the designated area.

The ensign smiled politely and indicated the readout. "As you see, sir, it's pointing you that way. Just follow the signals it will give you."

"Thank you, Ensign."

He walked away from her, and the ensign watched his departure with speculative eyes. "My pleasure, sir," she said with a soft, vaguely hopeful smile.

As Riker moved along the corridor, the black surface of another computer panel came alive with a flashing direction signal pointing ahead. "The next hatchway on your right," the computer directed.

He responded automatically. "Thank you."

"You're more than welcome, Commander Riker," the computer replied.

Riker flashed a look at it and realized the computers on this ship were far more sensitive and—he hesitated as he acknowledged it—*perceptive* than he had imagined possible. If computers that were truly mere machines serving the crew and ship were that sophisticated, what could he make of one like Data?

He moved along to the next hatchway and paused before it. "If you care to enter, Commander—" the computer went on smoothly.

Riker tossed it an irritated look and snapped, "I do." The hatch immediately slid open to admit him, revealing a vista of wild and beautiful parkland. The rich vegetation and trees were a lush green and grew in glades and dells where their coolness invited one to linger. A small stream meandered through the middle distance, and the wooded parkland seemed to stretch for miles to the horizon. The creamy clouds of a classic "buttermilk sky" streamed across the blue overhead. Off to Riker's left, he heard the distinct call of a crow over the general twitter of smaller birds in the trees. He smiled as a hummingbird whizzed past him to hover delicately over a flowering shrub nearby. He had seen holodecks before that attempted to do what this one accomplished so superbly. If he had not known exactly where he was, he would have believed absolutely that he was on Earth. *It's another machine,* his brain reminded him.

Then, over the bird song and the raspy chitter of squirrels in the trees, he heard someone whistling. He recognized the tune, which was being executed in a rather poor and laborious manner. It was an ancient one he had been taught as a child, and he shook his head as the final notes flatted. Riker pinpointed the source of the sound as coming from ahead and to his right, and he moved toward it. As he walked, he heard the whistling start again, still labored and frequently flat.

He paused at the top of the low hill overlooking the tumbling stream and scanned for the whistler. The sound seemed to be coming from the opposite bank, but the trees and heavy brush still screened the view. "Hello!" Riker called. The whistling continued.

The stream conveniently had a number of wide flat rocks that could be used to cross it. Riker started across, stepping easily from stone to stone with his long stride. The next to last one rocked loosely as his foot came down on it, and he brought his other foot up to it and swayed precariously for a moment before he caught his balance. Once he steadied, he was able to step to the final stone and to the shore. Peculiar that so perfect a holo projection should have a loose stone in the stream—and yet, it was the kind of thing one might find in a real creek. He decided the designer of the projection had programmed in "flaws" that nature might have contained.

He hesitated on the bank, readjusting his direction as the offkey tune persisted. Then he started up the path that threaded through the dense shrubbery. It led him to a wooded glade where deep purple violets and green jack-in-the-pulpits grew shyly in the cool shade of the trees. *Programmed for spring,* Riker noted absently.

The whistler had started the old tune again, and

Riker followed the sound up to where a sturdy tree forked to form a deep "Y" with its branches. Data was perched there, his lips pursed as he vainly tried to get the last notes correct. They tumbled out of key again. Apparently whistling was a difficult art for a machine to master. Riker quickly whistled the last bar correctly, and the android stared around blankly. Realizing who it was, he swung his legs around and dropped down to face the first officer.

"Marvelous how easily humans do that," he said with admiration. "I still need much practice. Was there something you wanted, sir?"

"There are some puzzles down on the planet that Captain Picard wants answered."

"Yes, the reports in regard to the Bandi and the construction of the station are quite incomplete."

"He suggested I take you on the away team I'll be leading."

"I shall endeavor to function adequately, sir."

Riker studied the android, who stared back at him, patiently waiting for him to go on. "I'm sure you will." Riker hesitated and then said, "He also suggested that I look up your record."

"Yes, sir. A wise procedure always. I am not known to you, and you would wish to acquaint yourself with my capabilities and areas of expertise."

Riker shifted uncomfortably. Why did this man— *machine*—put him so offguard? Data's manner was mild, and his voice was gentle and polite. Not obsequious, not overeager to please—simply matter of fact. His face had a range of expression, but Riker had a feeling it would never register extremes of any kind.

"The record says you were found on a planet which

had suffered a total biological catastrophe that destroyed all life on it."

"That is correct, sir."

"The planet was an Earth colony."

"Yes, sir."

"But you told me you were built by an alien race."

"That is also correct," Data replied calmly. "It occurred on Kiron III, where a human colony there faced accidental extinction. Unknown to that colony, an alien race of highly advanced machines lived there too. Seeing that the humans were to be destroyed, the aliens built me. They wanted to preserve what they considered the most important quality of the humans —their knowledge. Being machines themselves, they naturally considered information the most important quality of all. It appears I was completed and programmed shortly before the final catastrophe."

"What happened?"

"I am afraid I don't know, sir. I have a conscious memory only of what happened *after* everyone was dead. Someone had set a repeating distress beacon in orbit. A Starfleet vessel finally responded and discovered I was the only one alive on the planet. Humans are the first sentient life form I ever met." He smiled a little shyly. "I was taken to Earth for study by Starfleet, but in the question of how the catastrophe occurred or what its trigger was, I have no programmed information."

"The aliens?"

"Their fate is also a mystery to me. Apparently, they died as well."

"Odd that they built you in the shape of the humans and not themselves."

"Perhaps they felt that humans would relate better to me this way. At least, they built me to approximate what they judged to be human form."

"Mmmm." Riker looked at Data's yellow eyes and opalescent-gold skin, the only two features he could see that signaled that he was not human. "You are biomechanical in construct. Does that mean you eat?"

"I can consume almost any kind of solid material and convert it to fuel, and my systems do require oxygen for certain chemical balances. Ordinary liquids are of no use to me, which was why I was puzzled when the admiral insisted on trying to press a drink on me."

"Don't worry about that." Riker smiled. "That's just the admiral."

"Yes, sir, I understand," Data said eagerly. "Perhaps you can explain something else to me. Do you understand why he kept calling me 'boy'? Of course, I *was* designed as a fully functional male."

Riker cleared his throat, unsure of what to reply to that. "I believe . . . it's just an expression the admiral uses for any male younger than he is."

"Ah." As far as Data was concerned, that answered that.

Riker was still uncomfortable and decided to push the conversation into areas in which he had concerns. "You have the rank of lieutenant commander. Honorary, of course."

Data shook his head and replied cheerfully, "No, sir. Starfleet Academy class of '78; honors in probability mechanics and exobiology."

The android smiled at Riker's expression of surprise. "Actually, sir, Starfleet regulations allow the acceptance of any qualified candidate so long as he, she or it tests out as a sentient life form. Does any of this trouble you?" asked Data.

"To be honest . . . yes, a little."

Data nodded sagely. "Understood, sir. Prejudice is very human."

"Now *that* troubles me. Do you consider yourself superior to us?"

"I *am* superior in many ways. But—" Data hesitated. "I would gladly give it up to be human."

Riker studied him a moment, analyzing his own emotions. The fact Data was an android seemed less and less important in the face of his open honesty, his gentle philosophy, and his obvious yearning to become more than a bio-mechanical construct. Finally Riker said, "Nice to meet you—Pinocchio." Data stared at him, uncomprehending. "A joke," Riker explained.

"Ah! *Intriguing,*" Data said. "You must explain it to me."

Riker grinned spontaneously. "You're going to be an interesting companion, Data." Aware of the time, he added, "We should go back. The captain will want the away team to get started as soon as possible."

They walked back along the path that Riker had followed to the glade. Riker looked around again at the incredibly convincing foliage and shook his head. "This is marvelous," he said. "The *Hood* had a holodeck, but it was nothing like this. I understand it can be programmed in almost endless combinations."

"Yes, sir. Some seem to be requested more than others. For instance, this woodland pattern is quite popular. Perhaps because it duplicates Earth so well, coming here almost . . . makes me feel as if I'm human too."

Riker paused and picked up a long blade of grass to study. "I didn't believe these simulations could be so real."

"Much of it *is* real, sir. If the transporters can convert our bodies to an energy beam, then back to the original pattern again—"

"Yes, of course." Riker pointed the blade of grass. "The rocks and vegetation here have much simpler patterns. I saw a hummingbird on my way in . . . and I heard squirrels and a crow. . . ."

"Projections, sir." Data waved his hand at a nearby area. "The rear wall."

Riker stopped and stared intently. The wooded area stretched away in a dense growth of trees, low brush and shrubs. A few spots of color were visible where wildflowers spread a throw rug of blossoms on the grassy stetches. "I can't see it."

"We are practically next to it." The android bent and picked up a large rock as Riker squinted vainly to see the wall. He pitched the rock about eight feet in a line directly ahead of Riker. The stone hit *something* in midair with a heavy thud and then bounced back to fall in the thick grass. "Right there, sir," Data said helpfully.

"Incredible." Riker knew he had twenty/twenty vision, but stare as he might, he could not make out the wall that confined the holodeck. Wesley's voice in the near distance brought Riker around as the boy called out.

"Isn't this great?"

Wes was hurrying down the opposite slope toward

the stream. "This is one of the simple patterns, Commander Riker. They've got *thousands* more, some you just can't believe." He started across the creek, nimbly bouncing from rock to rock. "I was just over in the Himalayas, tracking the Yeti—"

Riker suddenly remembered the stone that had wobbled perilously under his feet when he had crossed. "Careful," he yelled, "that next rock is loose!"

Wes stepped on the slab, and it tipped sharply under him. His arms flailed, and he fell off balance, tumbling into the stream with a huge splash. Data bounded down the hillside in swift, ground-covering leaps, landed with perfect balance on the treacherous rock, and reached down to grab the front of the boy's tunic. Riker stared in amazement as the android easily lifted Wesley out of the water with one hand and hoisted him overhead.

Wes shook the wet hair out of his face and stared at Data in awe. *"Wow!"* he gasped. Data smiled faintly and set him down on a dry rock. "You must be the android. I mean, *sir* . . . uh, thank you. I can swim, but—"

"The water is ten degrees centigrade to simulate a mountain stream. I believe you should return to your quarters and change into dry clothes as soon as possible. It is an old Earth remedy for such an event."

"I'd have to agree, Wes," Riker said. He saw the plea dancing in the boy's eyes and knew what he would have wanted at that age. "Lieutenant Commander Data," he said formally, "may I present Wesley Crusher."

"How do you do, Mr. Crusher," Data said. He

offered his hand and lightly but firmly shook the boy's. Wesley loved it. Now *he* had an adventure to tell Adam and Craig Harris.

The intricate hatchway from Holodeck area 4-J into the corridor slid smoothly open at their approach. Data, Riker, and a very soggy Wesley stepped through. The boy was happily trailing behind a dirty wake of muddy water as he listened to the two officers talk.

Picard was on his way through the holodeck with Commander Reasons of Stores and Supply when the three figures emerging from the parkland area caught his eye. Two of them were instantly recognizable as Riker and Data. The wet and bedraggled boy was unknown to him, but he was clearly making a mess on the scrupulously clean deck. Reasons paused and looked inquiringly at him, and Picard motioned him ahead. "Go on, Mark. I'll meet you in the Stores office." Picard waited for the other three to approach him.

Wesley cringed inside, aware of his dripping clothes, his squelching shoes, and the long snake of muddy footprints he was leaving behind. There was no doubt in his mind as to the identity of the intimidating man with the severe eyes who waited for them at the corridor intersection. Even if he hadn't immediately recognized the four small gold disks of a Starfleet captain, he had seen the holo of his mother and father and Jean-Luc Picard often enough. As they halted in front of the captain, Wes would have liked to wish himself away—but there he had to stand, his wet clothes steadily forming a puddle on the deck around his feet.

"I'm glad we met you, Captain," Riker said. I was going to report as soon as I returned to the bridge." He glanced at Data and then met Picard's eyes again. "I investigated the subject you recommended. Most informative, sir."

"I'm glad you found it instructive, Commander," Picard said. His eyes tracked down to the puddle at Wesley's feet.

"Yes, sir," Riker continued. "Data has agreed to join my away team. I've decided to include Lieutenant Yar and Lieutenant Commander Troi."

"An excellent choice."

Wesley shrank inwardly as he felt the water dripping off him in what seemed like a river. *It's only a few drops,* he kept telling himself. And he knew very well that even one drop on Picard's deck was an offense to the captain.

"I have one other suggestion, sir. There's a young lieutenant who reported on board with me. According to his medical record, he has some interesting visual capabilities that might be of help to us. His name is LaForge."

"Very good." Picard lowered another glance toward the puddle collecting around Wesley's feet.

Wes cleared his throat and managed to say humbly, "Sir, maybe I should get something to wipe this water up."

"Good idea," Picard replied coolly. He turned and strode away.

Wesley continued to drip.

Wes found his mother in sickbay and begged a towel from her. Once he had mopped up the entire muddy trail he had left from the holodeck to sickbay, he dried himself off in Beverly's office while he regaled her with his adventures.

". . . and there's a low gravity gymnasium too. Did you know they have a pair of Sondrian marsh boars on the ecology deck? It would be hard to get bored on this ship—"

"All I want to know is how you got so wet." Beverly picked up another soggy towel coated with mud streaks. "Look at this mess."

"I couldn't help it, Mom. The rock I stepped on tipped and I fell in the stream and Commander Data had to pull me out."

She went back to the medical supplies check she was running to establish the state of her inventory on hand. "I'm sure there's a long tale that goes with that synopsis. Do I get to hear it at dinner?"

"Yes, ma'am."

"Good. Now go and clean yourself up properly."

"Okay." He looked up at her hopefully, deciding to ask for the favor that he had been mulling over since the day before. "Mom . . . could you get me a look at the bridge?"

"That's against the captain's standing orders. Unless there's a medical emergency or the captain specifically requests me to report, even I'm not welcome on the bridge."

"Are you afraid of the captain, too?"

Beverly turned on him, her cheeks flaming with color. "I certainly am *not!*"

"But Captain Picard *is* a pain, isn't he?"

Beverly paused and weighed her answer carefully. It would be easy to agree, to get Wes out of her hair for a while. But she had always been aware of her responsibilities as a single parent and had tried to answer her son's questions honestly. "Your father liked him very much. Great explorers . . . great captains . . . are often lonely . . . no chance to have a family. . . ."

"Just a *look,* Mom. I could stand in the turbolift and just get a *peek* when the doors open. The doors are going to open and close anyway, right? I won't get off."

"You're looking for trouble, Wes," Beverly said ominously. Then she glanced at him and saw the very real *want* in his eyes. She sighed. *Never could deny him much.* "Let's see what we can do."

Chapter Eight

GEORDI LAFORGE WAS startled to hear his name called over the intership. "Lieutenant LaForge, please report to First Officer Riker in Transporter Room Three. Lieutenant LaForge to Transporter Room Three immediately."

Hughes stared at him in equal surprise. "What's he want you for?"

"I don't know. But I'd better get to Transporter Room Three."

"What about Commander Barton? He wanted us to report at 1300. It's almost that now."

Geordi shrugged. "First officer ranks him."

When he arrived at the Transporter Room, Geordi found Riker waiting with two services officers and a sciences officer. He came to attention in front of Riker and announced formally, "Lieutenant LaForge reporting as ordered, sir."

"Right, LaForge. You're beaming down with us on an away mission. This is Commander Data, Commander Troi and Lieutenant Yar."

Geordi acknowledged the senior officers, a little uncomfortable with so much rank, then he looked back at Riker. "Sir, I'm supposed to report to Commander Barton—"

"We're aware of that. Captain Picard will clear it with the commander. On the platform, Lieutenant."

Geordi quickly took a place on the transporter pad with the others. "Could I ask what my assignment will be, sir?"

"I need your eyes, Lieutenant." Riker nodded to the transporter chief. "Energize."

They materialized near the foyer into the shopping area. The mall was crowded with off duty *Enterprise* personnel and civilians browsing and shopping. The Bandi were busy catering to their visitors, and Riker even noted that most of them looked decidedly happy instead of merely accommodating.

Tasha sent a practiced eye around the mall and moved up beside Riker briskly. "Recommend that someone begin by examining the underside of the station, sir. If this place was built the way most of them are, there'll be service tunnels under the whole complex. Sometimes looking at the underside gives you a better view of the top."

"Our sensors do show some passages down there, sir. Perhaps you and I?" Troi accompanied the suggestion with a slightly arch glance that carried another suggestion entirely. Riker looked away, troubled.

"Tasha—you and the counselor."

"Sir." Tasha strode away quickly. Troi shot Riker another look, one that was somewhat amused, and then followed her.

Riker turned to Geordi and Data and gestured them after him. "Let's start with the topside. Lieutenant LaForge."

"Sir, I still don't understand exactly what I'm looking for."

"There are a lot of questions about the construction of the station, Mr. LaForge," Data explained. The most basic appear to be how the Bandi built it so quickly and what materials they used."

"Take a good look around you, Lieutenant. Do you see anything unusual about the structural materials?"

Geordi began to scan, moving his head slowly. The VISOR allowed him to adjust his vision in a number of ways, microscopically, telescopically, and thermal register among others.

"Well, Lieutenant?" Riker prompted.

Geordi looked back at Riker and Data, shaking his head. "I can't see through solid matter, sir, but the material so far looks very ordinary. Alloys, pure metals, woods, plasticrete, synthetics. They all read the way they should."

Data's eyebrows lifted slightly. "An intriguing ability, Lieutenant. Are you positive they're all natural materials?"

"Except for the synthetics, sir."

"And it is not an illusion? It is real?" Riker asked.

"Yes, sir. No doubt about it."

Riker was disappointed, but it was too early to be discouraged. "Thank you, Lieutenant. I think you should join Lieutenant Yar and Commander Troi and do the same type of scan in the area they're investigating. Data, with me, please."

As they moved away, Geordi touched his communicator. "LaForge to Yar. Location, please."

Riker led Data toward the back of the mall where it connected with the old city. "Data, are you familiar with the information the Bandi filed with Starfleet when they applied for official station status?"

"Yes, sir. The *Enterprise* has a copy of it in her record banks. I am able to repeat it back to you file for file if you wish."

"I wish. Station construction materials."

Data seemed to look into himself briefly, then his eyes focused; and he said, "There were detailed architect's drawings and blueprints, but no requisitions for building materials were presented. No manufacturing orders."

"The first contact team reported that the Bandi had no known factories or laboratories to produce such materials, but they did have luxurious trade goods to offer. Everything the contact team could think of."

"It is possible they have factories hidden underground, undetectable by our scanners."

Riker tapped his communicator and spoke softly. "Yar."

"Yar here," Tasha responded crisply.

"The Bandi may have concealed laboratories or factories on the station's lower levels or beneath the old city. Keep an eye out for accessways, ventilation shafts, equipment ramps, anything that would indicate an industrial or technological center down there."

"Yes, sir."

Tasha looked around as Geordi joined her and Troi, his boots clattering on the access ladder he used to descend from the overhead hatch. As he dropped down the last few rungs, he grinned at the two women. "Commander Riker thought my eyes might come in handy down here."

"I was just going to contact him when he signaled," Tasha said. "What do you think of this?" She waved her hand around, directing Geordi's gaze to the tunnel.

Geordi whistled softly. "What *is* this stuff?"

The service tunnel walls were not at all what one would expect to find. They were smooth with faintly rounded surfaces that showed distinctive markings of unknown significance; and they glistened, picking up a glow from the dim light in the tunnel and reflecting it back.

"My question exactly," Tasha said.

Geordi scanned the surfaces closely. "These walls are something I've never seen before."

"Report to the commander," Troi said. "He will want to know this."

Tasha tabbed her communicator again. "Team Leader, we've found something interesting."

"Location?" Riker's voice inquired.

"We're in a passageway directly under the central mall area, sir. Lieutenant LaForge is studying the structural material here, but he says he's never seen anything like it."

"How are you examining it, LaForge?"

"Microscopically, thermally, how it reflects the electromagnetic spectrum. None of it is familiar. Very puzzling, sir."

Riker's voice was thoughtful. "Puzzling. A good word for it, Lieutenant. How about you, Troi? Are you sensing anything unusual?"

Troi frowned as she activated her communicator. She was reluctant to answer because she knew what he would ask of her, and she did not look forward to complying. "Sir, I've avoided opening my mind. Whatever I sensed in the *groppler's* office became very uncomfortable."

"I'm sorry, Counselor." Riker's voice was soft but insistent. He understood the courage it took for her to do this. "We need more information."

"Yes, sir. I understand." Troi glanced at Tasha and Geordi. Tasha was sympathetic, but she could never really grasp what occurred when Troi lowered the barriers she carefully kept in place. Young LaForge might comprehend it a little better. His eyesight was enhanced mechanically as her sensitivities and mental perceptions were enhanced telepathically. Perhaps he could understand how she sometimes resented the "gift" of that enhancement.

Slowly, Troi thinned the mental shielding she maintained. There were many minds around her, each with its own busy thoughts. She could not "read" the content of those thoughts, merely the feelings that accompanied them. The wash of emotions she sensed now was normal, with a few strong peaks of feeling pushing up here and there: LaForge's curiosity and farther away, on the very specific emotional band that was Riker, his concern. A smile twitched her mouth. She would have recognized his mental emanation anywhere, so closely attuned had they been.

Tasha was watching her closely, impatient for action. Suddenly, Troi emitted a short, sharp scream and sank to her knees. "Such pain," she gasped. Tasha leapt in beside her, a supporting arm around her shoulders. Troi swayed under the feelings of agony that buffeted her mind. "Pain . . . pain. . . ."

Vaguely she could hear Riker's voice over her communicator. "Hang on, I'm coming. *Enterprise*, lock us onto her signal!"

Geordi had joined Tasha, trying to comfort Troi. She could hear the murmur of their voices, but the pain gripped her mind so deeply, she was forced to shut them out while she tried to close her sensitivities off again. She had managed to pull the barriers almost all the way back when the transporter beam began to sparkle in the air near them, and Data and Riker slid into solid form.

Riker strode quickly to Troi, taking her hands gently and helping her to her feet. "I'm sorry. Can you close out the pain?"

Troi nodded, leaning against him for a moment. The woman in her drew strength from his loving concern. She pushed that revelation aside for the moment, and the professional in her took over. "Report, sir," she began. "I—"

"What was it?" Riker coaxed. "Was it just pain or—?"

"No—more than that. Unhappiness . . . terrible despair."

"Who?" he asked.

"I don't know! No life form anything like us. Not the Bandi either. Their mind patterns are completely different from what I felt."

"Then who is in pain?" Data asked thoughtfully.

Riker shook his head and looked around at the glowing walls. "What in hell kind of place is this?"

The *Enterprise* bridge was only nominally manned. Picard almost felt as if he had it to himself. Worf was hunched at the Ops panel at the front of the bridge, but the few other station keeping crew personnel worked quietly at the aft stations, routinely monitoring ship's systems. Picard had felt too edgy to stay cooped up in his ready room waiting for the away team's report. The spacious bridge at least gave him room to pace if he felt like it. The sound of the aft turbolift doors opening automatically brought his head around to see who it was. Picard stiffened in his chair as he realized what he was looking at.

Beverly Crusher stood just inside the turbolift door. She was caught squarely by Picard's dark look as he frowned at her and at Wes, who stood beside her in the lift. She shot a swift glance at her son. He was staring out in wonder and awe at his dream place, taking in as much as he could possibly see in this one brief and limited view. Beverly started to step forward onto the bridge, gesturing to Wes to stay in the turbolift. *Better get this over with,* she thought.

She had a nice little speech she had thought up and a decent reason for her to personally come to the bridge to speak to Picard rather than to merely report to him over the intership. She had discovered a serious shortage in one of their essential medical supplies. Her inventory check had uncovered the fact the *Enterprise* was carrying an overabundant supply of vitamins and food supplements and was dangerously low on the elements to create artificial whole blood which might be required in an emergency. The error had apparently occurred due to the mislabeling of medical containers at their original supply point. This was a mistake that had to be rectified as soon as possible, and she was justified in bringing it to Picard's attention.

"Permission to report to the captain. . . ." Beverly began.

Picard's cool voice dropped the bridge temperature at least ten degrees. "Children are *not* allowed on the bridge, Doctor."

Beverly stopped in her tracks. She admitted to herself she knew this could be trouble when she decided to do it, but still he *was* being just a little too hardnosed. "I respectfully point out, sir, that my son is not *on* the bridge. He merely accompanied me to it."

Picard hesitated. *"Your* son?" This was the boy he had seen with Riker and Data—dripping an unholy mess of mud and water on the holodeck.

"His name's Wesley. You saw him years ago when . . ."

"Oh," Picard said abruptly. "Yes." He remembered seeing the child when he brought her husband's body back.

The boy who stood in the turbolift, his eyes wide as an owl's, seemed small for his age—he'd be about fifteen—but he sported a hint of the auburn hair that crowned his mother's head. He had her fine features, too—not much of Jack in him except the vividly intelligent hazel eyes. And if Jack were still alive, would Picard have allowed his son on the bridge, as a courtesy to a man he had respected and cherished as a friend?

Picard cleared his throat. "Well—as long as he's here. . . ." Wesley's hopeful eyes nailed his, the plea standing in them loud and clear. Beverly waited.

Picard shrugged and tried to make his voice warmer, friendlier. "I knew your father, Wesley. Would you like to take a look around?" The boy was out of the turbolift in one swift step. "But don't touch anything," Picard added quickly.

The bridge was far bigger than Wes thought it would be. Even the viewscreen was larger than any he had ever seen before. The serenely operating stations on this level above the command well almost drew him, but his mother moved down the ramp toward Picard, and he obediently went with her. He was careful to set his feet down just *so* with every step so he didn't ruffle the carpet—or the captain.

Picard stood up and moved a little away from the command chair as Beverly and Wesley reached him. What would the boy want? Well, what would *he* have wanted at that age and in such a situation? He gestured slightly toward the command chair. "Try it out. For a minute."

Wesley's face lit and glowed like a million candle-power searchlight. He edged himself into the seat and ran his eyes over the chair arm panels.

Picard leaned forward and pointed proprietarily as he detailed each item. "The panel on your left is for log entries, library-computer access and retrieval, viewscreen control, intercoms, and so on. Don't touch anything."

"No, sir." Wesley gestured to the right chair arm panel. "On here, backup conn and Ops panels, plus armament and shield controls."

"Careful of those."

"Yes, sir." Wes stared around admiringly. "This ship is really carrying *weight*."

Picard glanced at Beverly, then back to Wes, perplexed. "I take it that's a compliment?"

Beverly nodded, smiling slightly. "In the current vernacular, it's—"

"The *best,*" Wes interjected. "She's beautiful, sir."

"I see. Thank you," Picard said dryly. "You might be interested in the forward viewscreen. It's controlled from the Ops position—"

Wesley picked it up eagerly. "—using the outboard, ultra-high resolution, multi-spectral imaging sensor systems, selecting any desired magnification."

"How do you know that, boy?" Picard snapped. This child was altogether too clever.

Before Beverly or Wes could respond, a distinctive signal sounded on the command chair's left-hand panel. The boy instinctively, almost casually, reached out and tabbed one of the controls on the arm panel. "Perimeter alert, Captain!" And as he realized what he had done, he was instantly mortified.

Beverly's face flamed in embarrassment, and Picard was furious. Three voices began indignantly at the same time.

"Wes, you shouldn't have touched that."

"I'm sorry!" Wesley said, jumping up out of the chair. "I didn't mean to. I just *knew how.*"

"Off the bridge, both of you." Picard growled.

At the Ops console, Worf was staring around at them, not sure what to do. The signal had to be answered, but the captain seemed to be . . . involved.

Beverly pushed Wes toward the turbolift, looking back at Picard. "I'm so sorry. . . ."

"He was told not to touch anything."

The signal came again, and Worf decided he should say something. "Perimeter alert, sir."

Beverly stopped and swung around to face Picard.

Wesley might have offended the captain, but she was damned if she'd let him take any blame when he had been right. "As my son tried to tell you!" she said sharply. Then, head high, she marched into the forward turbolift with Wesley and snapped, "Quarters Deck 3."

As the doors closed behind them, Picard slammed his right fist into his open palm, frustrated. Then he jumped for his chair to key open his comm line as the signal came again. "This is Picard."

The assistant security chief's voice boomed over the intership. "Ship's sensors have detected the presence of a vessel approaching Deneb IV. No other ship is scheduled to arrive at this time, sir."

"Could it be the *Hood* returning?"

"The vessel does not match the *Hood*'s configuration or tonnage, sir."

"Worf, put it on the main screen."

Worf quickly tabbed his Ops panel. The huge screen in front of Picard instantly flashed on the image of a ship. It was at far range; but even on the standard scale, it was big, dark, and ominous. It had only a few running lights, and its somber hull reflected very little starshine. In fact, it seemed to absorb light. Even the gleam of Deneb IV's sun only showed it as a shadow swiftly moving against the galactic panorama behind it. It was approaching very quickly.

"Identification?" Picard snapped.

Worf was ready, but the answers weren't good. "Vessel unknown. Configuration unknown. Origin unknown, sir."

"Hail it!"

"I've been trying, sir. Automatic ID sent with request for same. No response."

"Raise all shields, Lieutenant."

Worf's hands moved on the panel. "Shields up, sir. Full power."

"Phasers ready."

"Phasers charged and ready, sir." This from the security officer at the Weapons and Tactics station behind him.

"Sound yellow alert."

The alert signal pounded through the ship, and duty personnel efficiently began to arrive on the turbolifts and take their stations. Picard studied the still advancing vessel. He had never seen anything like this either, but that didn't mean it could not belong to a race they *did* know. "Get me *Groppler* Zorn, Lieutenant. Continue universal greetings on all frequencies."

Worf tabbed his panel. There was a sharp *beep,* and then Zorn's voice echoed on the bridge.

"Yes. This is *Groppler* Zorn, Captain."

Picard didn't waste time on the niceties. Whatever this ship was, he had a gut-deep feeling it was not here on a peaceful mission. Was this *Q* at work—or was it someone else? "There is an unidentified vessel rapidly approaching this planet. It refuses to respond to hails. Do you know who it is?"

"There are no ships scheduled to arrive until—"

"I asked you if you knew who it is, *Groppler.* You mentioned the Ferengi Alliance to me."

Zorn's voice trembled nervously. "Ah. Yes. But we have had no dealings with them, Captain. It was only a—a thought."

"Are you sure that's all? Or did you send out a message for a rendezvous with one of the Ferengi vessels? Perhaps one you now regret sending?"

"No." Zorn sounded desperate. "Captain, I prom-

ise you it was an empty threat. I wanted your cooperation, your endorsement to Starfleet. Forgive me—"

"The vessel has reached orbital insert trajectory,
sir," Worf reported. "Sensors say it measures twelve
times our volume."

"What could they want?" Zorn wailed. He knew the
size and tonnage of the *Enterprise*. Anything so much
larger than that was a horrendous threat to the station
and the Bandi.

"They won't talk to us to let us know," Picard
replied coolly.

"Captain, can't you force them to identify themselves? If they are hostile—"

"We'll defend you as best we can, *Groppler*. Picard
out."

"What if it's *Q*, sir?"

That thought still rode Picard's mind. He shook his
head. "I expect he'll make himself known as he did
earlier. But that's not the vessel we encountered
before."

As they tensely watched the viewscreen, the huge
ship approached and settled into geosynchronous
orbit somewhat above and to starboard of the *Enterprise*. Picard could almost feel the oppressive weight
of the massive vessel pressing down on them. Suddenly a glowing pulse of light throbbed from the underside of the mystery ship toward the *Enterprise*.

The light flared over everything and everyone on
the bridge. Picard twisted his head and saw the details
of both objects and people outlined in a spectacular
glow. Crew personnel were startled, but no one
seemed to be in pain or discomfort.

The light faded slowly away, and Picard tabbed on

his intership line. "All stations—damage reports." He glanced around the bridge swiftly. "Status report."

"No apparent damage, sir," Worf said.

The others confirmed quickly. Every station reported the glow, but no damage. No casualties. All ship's functions were unimpaired and operating normally.

"Science—analysis of what hit us."

The science officer checked his console readings. "Nonmechanical probe, sir. Possibly sensory or telepathic in nature."

Worf looked up from his Ops panel again. "Sensors confirm we were just scanned, sir."

Chapter Nine

THE UNDERGROUND SERVICE tunnel felt oppressive despite its size. The strange, smooth, shining walls with their curious markings gleamed in the soft light from an undetectable source. Troi was not aware of the sensation or of her companions as she leaned against the wall, still concentrating on the empathic waves impinging on her mind. Riker watched her, knowing she had shut them out and was allowing someone else to "walk" within the lanes of her mind. Geordi was closely examining the wall surfaces and Data was trying to raise the *Enterprise*.

Tasha moved in beside Troi and touched her shoulder. "Pain again?" Straightforward and honest, Tasha understood intellectually that Troi was a kind of receiver for the emotional emanations of others; but because she could never receive them herself, she did not *know* what it was Troi felt or perceived.

"Troi, you've been at it enough!" Riker snapped.

"No," she said, shaking her head. "I feel close to an answer of some kind. There is . . . deep need . . . hunger." Tears sprang to her dark eyes, and she impatiently brushed them away.

Data had been steadily calling the *Enterprise* on every frequency the communicator offered. He turned to Riker, somewhat perplexed. "Commander, something is shielding our communicators."

"Are we too far underground?"

"No, sir. The effective range of the new communicator devices is well beyond this, and ordinary tunnel construction materials should not interfere."

"This isn't ordinary construction material," Geordi interjected.

Troi looked around at them, pulling her concentration back. One part of her mind had been listening to them, and she responded to both impressions, pulling it together. "That's *exactly* the feeling I've been reading," she said, nodding toward Data. "As if someone doesn't want us to be in touch with our ship."

"Come *on*," Riker said. "Let's get to the surface."

The viewscreen pictured the intruder vessel as it hovered in near orbit with the *Enterprise*. It worried Picard—too big, too dark, too silent. "Worf—anything?"

The big Klingon shook his head. "We have scanned all known records, sir. We have nothing on any such vessel. Nothing even close."

Ops looked around quickly and informed Picard, "Still no response to our signals, sir. We've done everything but threaten them."

"Sensor scans, Mr. Worf."

"Our sensors seem to just bounce off, sir."

"Can you get any readings at all?"

"No readings, sir." Worf looked up at the dark and

oddly shaped ship on the viewscreen. "Who *are* they?"

Suddenly, a strange, blue-white beam snapped from the alien vessel down toward the surface. Another immediately followed. Worf reared around toward Picard, alarm etched on his broad, dark features.

"They're firing at Farpoint, sir!"

"Bring photon torpedoes to ready," Picard barked at the assistant security chief. "Damage report, Lieutenant Worf. That was directed at the station."

Worf tabbed controls on his console and reported over his shoulder. "No damage evident, sir. They've hit the old Bandi city—not the station."

In the service tunnel, Riker and his team had been hurrying along the passageway with Troi and Tasha in the lead. Riker noticed the smooth, rounded wall structure of the tunnel giving way to an ordinary rectangular corridor with a stone and tile cladding. He paused briefly to look closer at the area where the two blended imperceptibly. Glancing around to Geordi, Riker waved the young lieutenant closer; and LaForge moved in to examine the wall material.

"LaForge?"

"At this point, it becomes ordinary stone, sir. Matching what's above." His brows knit together in a puzzled frown. "Amazing seaming here. The two appear to just melt together."

"Those stairs ahead are where Tasha and I entered, sir," Troi interjected.

Riker could see the stone block steps about twenty meters ahead where the tunnel opened up. Suddenly there was a long rumbling explosion that sent them reeling as the ground bucked and shuddered around them. Tasha pulled herself together first. "Explosion. Phaser blast."

"Negative," Data said calmly. "But something similar."

"Location," Riker snapped.

Data scanned with his tricorder quickly and looked up. "One kilometer, two hectometers away. The old city." Another explosion rocked the area, the tremors shivering the ground under their feet.

Riker quickly glanced around to Troi. "Try to get through to the ship again. You, Yar and LaForge will beam up from here. Now!" Turning to Data, he nodded toward the stairway. "Data, with me. I want to see exactly what's happening." He started toward the steps, Data immediately following on his heels.

"Don't," Troi said involuntarily. Riker turned back. She knew she shouldn't, but she couldn't stop herself. Her mind flashed at his. *Don't. If you should be hurt—*

Riker's face turned to stone. "You have your orders, Commander! Carry them out!"

Chastened, Troi looked away, her face flaming. She read his anger, his own embarrassment at her flash of familiarity. "Yes, sir. I'm sorry." Riker and Data were already climbing the stairs toward the upper level as Troi reached up to tab her communicator. *"Enterprise, three to beam up."*

Riker and Data emerged in the shopping mall, which was in chaos. Although there was no damage here, the Bandi were fleeing it in panic. Another explosion ripped the air, and a cloud of dust from crumbling masonry puffed out the back of the mall where it connected to the old city. Riker nodded to Data, and they started for the damaged section on the run.

Mark Hughes had been assigned to assist the transporter chief in Transporter Room 7. He was a little annoyed to have to stand aside and look on while the chief went about his duties. Mark, after all, had had instruction at the Academy in the basic functions of the transporter; and his training sessions had earned him high marks. Still, he was just an ensign, newly signed on; and he knew he would have to serve an apprentice turn in every ship's department in his first year on board.

The chief received Troi's order and locked on to the three communicator signals at the Farpoint Station coordinates. "What're they doing below ground?" he wondered aloud. But he shrugged his shoulders and started the transport.

The sparkling shimmer of the collection and materialization began on the pad, and the three columns formed into the solid figures of Tasha Yar, Deanna Troi and Geordi LaForge. As they stepped off the platform, Hughes moved forward to his friend. Tasha ignored Hughes and said briskly over her shoulder, "Mr. LaForge. To the bridge, please."

"Yes, ma'am." Geordi hesitated and fell back a little behind the two women as Hughes stepped in beside him.

"Geordi, what's going on?" Hughes demanded. "You're no sooner on board and you're assigned to an away mission. Now they want you on the bridge—"

"Mr. LaForge," Tasha snapped as she looked back and realized he was not following her.

"Coming," Geordi said. He looked at Hughes, shrugged helplessly, and ran to catch up to the other two officers.

Hughes watched him out the Transporter Room door and then glanced back at the transporter chief. "Some people would do anything for the moon and the stars . . . and some have 'em dumped right in their laps without even having to ask." He felt jealous about Geordi's good fortune, although he had to admit Geordi did have some rank on him. *But not that much,* he thought a little bitterly. He was frank enough with himself to acknowledge he felt left out . . . not only of feeling a part of the crew but also because Geordi already seemed to be moving far ahead of him . . . maybe to a place where a friend who only ranked as a new ensign would not be wanted.

On the planet, Riker and Data had reached one of the boundaries that linked with old Bandi city with Farpoint Station. It was a courtyard, almost like a village square; but its pleasant aspect was ruined by the fire raging in a crumpled structure on the far side of it. A hand-worked metal door stopped the flow of traffic between the two sections, and when Data and Riker reached it, they found it was locked.

"Phaser it," Riker ordered. As Data adjusted his phaser to a cutting setting, the first officer touched his communicator and spoke. *"Enterprise,* this is Riker." There was no immediate response. Data briefly glanced up, then fired his phaser at the door's locking mechanism. The lock popped under the blast, and Data was able to wrestle the door open with a minimum of effort.

"Enterprise, come in," Riker said. He shook his head and followed Data through the door. "They must be busy up there—with whatever is—"

The explosive blast of some kind of energy bolt roared over his words. As Riker and Data whirled to look in the direction from which it had come, they saw another building shatter into stones and a ballooning cloud of dust. As the structure collapsed, Riker keyed his communicator again.

Picard studied the main viewscreen dispassionately. The mystery vessel directed another bolt of ferocious energy down at the planet, but even the maximum enlargement available on the screen was not able to give specific details. Worf was restless at the Ops console in front of him. Picard could see the Klingon's shoulder muscles bunching and tensing as he shifted weight in the chair. Finally, Worf grated insistently, "Standing by to fire, sir."

Picard waited for a full breath before he shook his head firmly. "Continue weapons standby. What exactly is that ship firing on?"

"Hard to tell, sir. *Looks* like only the old city, but some of the hits have been very close to where Farpoint Station joins it."

"No response from Riker yet?"

"No, sir. I have a continuous send for him. He might've gotten caught in some of that," Worf said, nodding at the viewscreen to indicate the damaged city.

Suddenly, Zorn's voice burst from the communications speaker. "Enterprise, Enterprise, *help us! Come in, please!"*

"Vessel firing again, sir," Worf rasped.

"What shall we do?" Zorn pleaded.

Picard tabbed the communications panel on his left. *"Groppler* Zorn—

"Captain! You must save us! We're under attack—we have casualties—"

"We will send assistance, *Groppler,"* Picard cut in harshly. "Where are the casualties?"

"The city," Zorn's voice wavered. The sound of another explosion almost obliterated his next words. "The city. Center of the city. Hurry, please!"

"At once," Picard snapped. He tabbed his communications line again. "Sickbay. Dr. Crusher."

Beverly's voice responded immediately. "Crusher here."

"The Bandi city is suffering casualties. We'll need an emergency medical team—"

"I'm on it now, sir. Crusher out."

Picard grunted approvingly. Then he addressed the communications line again. "Commander Riker, come in. Where are you?" The hiss of the turbolift doors opening signaled newcomers to the bridge. He glanced around to see Troi, Tasha and Geordi hurry onto the bridge. "Riker?" Picard asked quickly.

"Still planetside, sir," Troi replied.

"I see. Mr. LaForge."

"Sir."

"You're a conn officer, aren't you?" At Geordi's nod, Picard gestured toward the empty conn panel beside Worf. "Take that position now. We may have to maneuver in a hurry."

"Yes, sir." Geordi hurried forward to slide into the console seat. Behind them, Tasha relieved the assistant chief security officer on the Weapons and Tactical console. Troi moved to her seat on Picard's left.

"Where was Riker when you last saw him?" Picard began, to Troi.

Riker's own voice sharply cut in over the communications line. "Riker to *Enterprise.* Come in."

"Finally," Picard muttered. "Commander, where are you?"

"With Data, on the edge of the old city, Captain. It's being hit hard."

"So I hear. And Farpoint Station? Any damage there?"

There was another crash in the background before Riker's voice came through clearly. "Negative on damage to Farpoint, sir. Whoever they are, it seems they're carefully avoiding hitting the station."

"It's an unidentified vessel that's entered orbit with us here. No ID, no answer to our signals. . . ."

"They're hitting the Bandi city hard, sir. Heavy casualties very probable."

"Understood, Commander. Emergency assistance is underway." Picard paused, pursing his mouth. *A time for thought, and a time for action.* He said carefully, "Would you object to your captain ordering a clearly illegal kidnapping?"

"No objection, sir—if you feel it's necessary."

"I do. Zorn may have the answers we need. Bring him here!"

"Aye, sir!" Riker responded briskly. "Riker out."

"Mr. Worf, put our mystery vessel back on screen." Worf quickly complied, and the main viewscreen flashed up the image of the dark, ominous ship hovering over Farpoint. Picard studied it silently, unable to fathom its intent. He shook his head and turned to look at Troi. "Why are they only attacking the old city? If they have a quarrel with us, they would fire on us . . . or on the station that's supposed to be ours. Why limit it to the Bandi city?"

"Does it matter if they only have a quarrel with the Bandi?" Troi asked. "We have a moral obligation to defend those people."

"They're forcing a difficult decision on me, Counselor."

"I doubt protecting the Bandi would violate the Prime Directive. They've asked for our help. True, they are not actual allies. . . ."

"But we *are* in the midst of diplomatic discussions with them. We owe them this much." Picard spoke without looking around to Tasha. "Lock phasers on that vessel, Lieutenant."

Tasha's slim fingers moved purposefully on the panel. "Phasers locked on, Captain."

The flash of intense white light that bathed the bridge brought Picard out of his chair almost in a fighting stance. Of course, it would be *Q*. The creature wore the red and black judge's robes he had sported in the courtroom. He sneered around at Picard and the bridge crew, and his eyes rested with particular sarcasm on Tasha at the Weapons and Tactics console. "Typical, so typical," he said. "Savage life forms never follow even their own rules. Or the rules they *say* they have."

"What's that supposed to mean, *Q?*"

Q turned his attention back to Picard, and the corners of his mouth curled upward tauntingly. "I recall an impassioned speech—not too long ago— some young woman of my acquaintance. . . ." He shifted his eyes to Tasha again. "What was it now? Ah. 'This so-called court should get down on its knees to what Starfleet is, what it represents.' You remember that, don't you, Captain? And *you* had a statement to make yourself. Let's see. . . ." *Q* snapped his fingers. "Yes. 'We agree there is evidence to support the court's contention that humans have been savage. Therefore, I say "test us" . . . test whether this is *presently* true of humans.' I liked that, Captain. Very persuasive. So persuasive, in fact, that I returned you to your ship and allowed you to come here to be tested."

"Get off my bridge!" Picard roared.

Q smiled sadly and shook his head. "Interesting, that order about phasers."

"Still standing by on phasers, Captain," Tasha said coldly and briskly. *Q* flicked a look at her, but she ignored him and kept her eyes on Picard.

Q turned to Picard and held up his hands appealingly. "Please don't let me interfere." He dropped his voice to a deep, insinuating purr. "Use your weapons."

"With no idea of who's on that vessel, my order was a routine safety precaution. We have not been fired upon. The vessel is directing its attack on the Bandi city, and we do not know what state of hostility may exist between—"

Q rolled his eyes and broke into laughter. "Really? No idea of what that ship represents?" He shook his head. Truly, he could not comprehend the stupidity of these creatures. "The meaning of that vessel is as plain as—as plain as the noses on your ugly little primate faces. And if you were truly civilized, Captain, wouldn't you be doing something about the casualties occurring down there?"

So! Picard thought. *Maybe he doesn't know everything.* He tabbed the communication control on the armrest of his chair and snapped, "Captain to C.M.O. Are you reading any of this?"

Beverly's voice came back almost instantly in crisp response. "Medical teams already preparing to beam down, Captain. They will be in place in five minutes."

"Compliments on that, Doctor." Picard turned back to Q, who stood there grinning at him. "Any questions? Starfleet personnel are trained to render aid and assistance whenever—"

"Whenever you allow people to be harmed?"

"That's an unfair comparison," Picard said.

"Yes, but true. And I'll give you another unfair but true statement, Captain. Starfleet people *are not trained in clear thinking,* or you would have already realized what is happening and that the Bandi would have suffered no casualties at all if you had acted on the knowledge."

"Let's consider *your* thoughts. You call us 'savages' and yet you apparently *knew* those people down there would be killed and wounded. Why didn't you say something? Do something to stop it? Is 'testing us' worth that price in innocent lives? I say it is you whose conduct is uncivilized."

"Sir, they're firing on the planet again," Worf interjected.

The bridge crew looked up quickly at the main viewscreen in time to see the blue-white bolt arrow down toward the Bandi city again. To Picard's eyes, it struck the very center of the old complex. Another streak of energy swiftly pursued it.

"Go to impulse power! Position us between that vessel and the planet. Shields full on!"

"Aye, sir," Geordi snapped in quick response, his hands moving expertly on the conn panel. "Impulse power to—" He stopped, looking down, as the panel faded slowly into blackness. "We have no ship control, sir. *It's gone!*"

Riker and Data ran down the old city corridors toward Zorn's office. The transporter beam could have gotten them there instantaneously; but immediately after Riker had acknowledged Picard's order, the communications link between him and the *Enterprise* had gone silent again. Riker was in good condition, but he found himself straining for breath after the long run through the old city. Data, of course, had no such problem. Zorn's office was only a few feet in front of them when a tremendously strong energy bolt flared blue directly beside the door. The corridor rocked under the impact, and Riker and Data were flung to the floor. The ceiling cracked and partially collapsed, sending plaster dust and sand showering down on them. Once the debris stopped falling, Data stirred and sat up. Beside him, Riker slowly hauled himself upright, ducking as a fist-sized chunk of ceiling dropped to the ground.

"Are you undamaged, sir?" Data asked.

"Yes. You?"

Data's eyes seemed to glaze over as he ran an internal check. After a few seconds, he blinked and nodded to Riker. "All systems operating."

"Then let's go."

They got to their feet and moved toward Zorn's office. The door was hanging by its hinges, and debris dust drifted lazily through the room. It was badly damaged; apparently the last bolt or one shortly before had been a direct hit. Outside, the explosion of another energy bolt sounded with a distant boom.

Riker and Data ventured cautiously into the office, looking around in dismay at the shattered furniture. Only the beautiful desk seemed to have survived reasonably intact.

"Zorn?"

A muffled noise quavered from under the desk. Riker strode toward it quickly. *"Groppler* Zorn?" He found the old Bandi administrator cowering under the elegant desk, shaking and sobbing in fear. "Please come out, sir. We're beaming you up to the *Enterprise."* He reached under the desk and gently drew Zorn out and up to a standing position.

Zorn didn't seem to hear him as he looked up with pleading eyes. "Please. You can make it stop. Drive it away."

"Drive *what* away, *Groppler?"*

Zorn flinched, sucking in his breath as though realizing he had said something he shouldn't. "I don't know," he said quickly.

"Unlikely, sir," Data said flatly. He turned to Zorn. "Our records show that you supervised all Bandi contact with Starfleet. We can presume you did so with any other offworld contacts you have had."

"We haven't done anything wrong!"

"If that is so, you have nothing to fear. The *Enterprise* will be a safe shelter for you—"

"I have nothing to say to your captain."

"Then I'm afraid we'll have to leave. Goodbye, sir," Riker said firmly. He turned away, and Data wheeled around to follow him.

"No!" Zorn screamed in a frightened voice. He caught himself and brought himself under more control, and his voice only shook slightly as he went on, "No, don't leave. I . . . I'll try to explain some of—"

The air began to take on an eerie glow around Zorn. The *groppler* stared down at his body in horror.

"No," he screamed again. "No—"

Riker took a step forward, as the sparkling luminiscence completely covered the screaming Bandi administrator.

Zorn clutched at Riker's arm desperately. "Help me," he pleaded. "Help me!"

The glow began spreading over Riker's body. He felt a strange tingling creep down his arm . . .

"Sir, no!" Data grabbed Riker and pulled him back. The first officer was surprised to feel the immense power in Data's fingers, and equally surprised to realize the android had pulled him back with just two fingertips.

Zorn's screams stopped suddenly. Data and Riker glanced around.

Save for the two of them, the room was empty.

Chapter Ten

RIKER BLINKED, STARING at the space Zorn had occupied. Behind him, Data murmured, "I suspect this will create a difficulty."

"You have a talent for understatement, Commander." Riker tapped his communicator to key it and barked, "First officer to *Enterprise.*"

Picard's voice immediately crackled over the minute speaker. "Go ahead, Riker."

He's not going to like this, but I'm damned if I know what to do about it, Riker thought. He shook his head slightly, took a breath, and went ahead. "We've lost Zorn, sir. Something like a transporter beam has snatched him out of here."

"Like a transporter beam? Not one of ours?"

"I would say alien, sir," Data chimed in.

"Question, sir," Riker went on. "Could it have been this *Q?*"

Q's eyebrows lifted archly, and he smiled at Picard's sour expression. It was so plain, and these fools would never get it. *"None* of you knows who transported him? You're running out of time, Captain."

Troi moved in her chair, stirring from an inner-directed center of attention. She had been alert to Picard's hostility and *Q*'s mocking taunts until something *else* crept in, nudging her mind subtly. She frowned, analyzing it, separating out the elements. "Captain," she said finally, "suddenly I'm sensing something else." He swung around to look at her questioningly. "It's satisfaction, enormous satisfaction."

"Oh, very good," *Q* chuckled.

Picard ignored him. "From the same source as before?"

"No, that was on the planet. This is much closer."

The Captain turned toward the viewscreen where the mystery ship hovered ominously in orbit. *Q* rocked up on the balls of his feet and then back again to his heels, grinning wickedly at Troi. "Excellent, Counselor!" He jerked his head toward Picard. "He's such a dullard, isn't he?"

"Perhaps," Picard shot back. "But you seem to think this is nothing but a riddle game—and I'll remind you we have more serious business here."

A voice crackled over the intership, interrupting them. "Transporter Room 6 to captain. First officer and Mister Data have now beamed aboard. They're on their way to the bridge, sir."

"Ah," *Q* said, smiling cheerfully. "Excellent also! Perhaps with more of these little minds helping, you'll—"

Picard whirled on him, exploding. He seldom lost his temper, didn't believe it ever accomplished much. But this creature was too overbearing, too smug to be tolerated. "That is *enough*, damn it!"

Q stepped back slightly, his eyebrows cocked sardonically again. "Have you forgotten we have an agreement? I'm just urging you to keep it."

Picard was aware the turbolift doors had opened and someone entered the bridge. Data and Riker most likely. His attention remained riveted to the alien before him. *Q* had moved back, given ground. Picard's fencing training snapped to the fore, and he instinctively stepped forward. When an opponent has been forced back, follow; attack boldly. "We have an agreement which you are at this moment breaking by taking over my vessel, interfering with my decisions!" He was nose to nose with *Q,* and his voice rang with authority, though he did not raise it. "Either leave or finish us."

Q paused thoughtfully, studying Picard. Everyone else on the bridge found himself holding his breath, waiting to see how the mercurial alien would react. In fact, though Picard had surprised him with the vehemence of his attack, *Q* was enjoying himself. Finally, he allowed a sweet smile to cross his face; and his voice, when it came, was gentle. "Temper, temper, mon Captain. I am merely trying to assist a pitiful species toward a slight achievement before you have to return to your little planet—and stay there. Perhaps I'll leave if Commander Riker provides me with some amusement."

"Do nothing that he asks!" Picard snapped at Riker.

Riker had no intention of doing so and merely shot a confirming glance at his commander. *Q* moved toward him, his voice pleasant and persuasive. "But I ask so little. And it is necessary if you are to solve all this."

"What is it you want?" Riker asked.

Q flipped a casual hand toward the huge viewscreen and the alien ship. Beam over there with your . . ." He paused and turned to Picard appealingly, "What do you call it? Your away team?"

"I'll risk no lives on such an unknown," Picard said flatly.

The alien shook his head in great pity. Such a trial, these humans. They simply refused to let him help them. "You should already know what you'll find there, Captain. But perhaps it is too adult a puzzle for you. Too complex. Too far above your puny efforts . . ." He paused. "Maybe you should just use your phasers . . ."

"*Q*, I'm warning you . . ."

"Captain," Riker said. "With all due respect, I want to beam over there."

Q turned quickly toward Riker. "Ah! You show promise, my good fellow."

Riker interrupted angrily, nodding toward Picard. "Have you understood any part of what he's tried to tell you? Humanity is no longer a savage race!"

"What did they used to say, back in your 20th Century? Yes, I have it. 'Talk is cheap.' The words are very fine, my dear Commander Riker. But *you must still prove that!*" The blinding flash that signaled his departure exploded in their faces, and the officers shrank back from its brilliance.

Riker turned to Picard as the light died away, leaving their bridge looking almost faded in its soft light and muted colors. "Sir, I repeat my request to take an away team to that ship. If there are answers, that's where they'll be."

"I'm surprised you believe that, too," Picard said.

Riker lifted his shoulders in a shrug. "It's the only place left to look, sir. Why not?"

Picard turned it over in his mind. Riker was correct, of course; and Picard had known that he would agree to the first officer's request the moment he had made it. He nodded.

"If there's anything there, we'll find it, sir."

Picard nodded again and moved away up the ramp toward the aft turbolift doors. "Sir?" Riker persisted. "If he's not open to evidence in our favor, where will you go from there?"

Picard paused at the top of the ramp and turned to look back at Riker. "I'll be attending to my duties."

"To the bitter end."

The captain tilted his head, thinking about it. Then his mouth tilted in a half smile. "I see nothing so bitter in that." Riker nodded soberly, and then he offered a thumbs-up sign to Picard. The captain strode to the turbolift doors, which obligingly parted before him. "Sickbay," he said curtly, and the doors closed on him.

Riker decided he liked this man very much—and if they managed to get out of this, he thought he was going to enjoy shipping out under Captain Jean-Luc Picard's command.

Beverly Crusher had been busy running routine checks on the new personnel signing aboard, correlating their last recorded medical status with current readings. Lieutenant LaForge lay quietly on the examining table before her now. His full range scan showed him to be in excellent health, as his records stated. She was as interested in the visual prosthesis which lay beside him on the table as she was in his medical readouts. His blind eyes stared unblinkingly straight up into the overhead lighting; and she found the flat gray irises with no pupil somewhat disturbing. As she finished the scan of his eyes with her hand instruments, she said, "Naturally, I've read up on your case. You are able to compensate extremely well with the VISOR appliance—"

"Yes, a remarkable piece of bioelectronic engineering by which I 'see' much of the EM spectrum ranging from simple heat and infrared through radio waves, et cetera, et cetera," Geordi chanted in a bored lilt. "Forgive me if I've said it and listened to it a thousand times before."

"Your records indicate you've been blind all your life."

Geordi sat up at her tap on his shoulder and swung his feet over the side of the examining table. "Born this way," he replied flatly. It was a fact, one he lived with. Period. As he accepted the VISOR that gave him vision, he also accepted the fact that nature had seen fit not to allow him to see as other people did. Beverly lifted the device and placed it in his hands.

"And you've felt pain all the years you've used this?"

Geordi nodded philosophically. "They say it's because it uses my natural sensors in different ways."

Beverly hesitated thoughtfully. She could think of options but surely other people had proposed them too. The young lieutenant seemed resigned to the situation. Still, it was worth venturing them to him. "I see two choices. The first is painkillers. . . ."

"Which would affect how this works," Geordi interrupted. He slipped on the VISOR and looked at her directly. "No."

The doors to sickbay slid open, and Picard stepped in. Beverly shot a glance past Geordi and stiffened slightly when she saw the captain enter, then her attention was drawn back to LaForge's question. "Choice number two?"

"Exploratory surgery, desensitize the brain area troubling you."

Geordi slipped off the examination table and shook his head. That was one he had heard before, too; but he managed a smile at her. "Same difference. No thank you."

Beverly smiled back at him, understandingly. "Just thought I'd remind you the options are there. And I'm sure there will be others in the future."

"I'll keep an open mind, Doctor."

Picard stepped forward from the doorway, glancing between Beverly and the young lieutenant. "Any problems, Doctor? Lieutenant?"

"No, sir. Absolutely none at all," Geordi replied. He nodded to Beverly and moved toward the door.

Picard watched him out and then turned to Beverly as she spoke. "Can I help you, Captain?"

He was uncomfortable, but he was also a man who didn't like to leave things left unsaid to fester in silence. Better to state what was on his mind and have everything clear. "Just some unfinished business. I didn't want to have you thinking I was a cold-blooded bastard."

Beverly's right eyebrow arched, and she managed to conceal a smile; but the humor trickled into her voice anyway. "Now why would I ever think that?"

All right, she was laughing at him. Picard relaxed a little, realizing she was going to let him have his say. He had thought she might be rigid or hostile after their two confrontations; but she was proving to be not at all what he anticipated. That was interesting . . . He immediately stopped that line of thought and turned to what he had come for. "I didn't exactly welcome you aboard in the best personal or professional manner. I yelled at your son, who, as you pointed out, was quite correct in his assessment of the bridge situation. He does seem to have a good grasp of starship operations. I apologize for shouting at him. I . . . ah, don't have a great deal of experience with children."

Beverly smiled at him then, accepting the apology. "I can understand that, Captain. I assure you neither of us were permanently damaged by the encounter."

Picard considered the statement a moment and finally extended his hand to her. "Then, welcome aboard, Doctor. I hope we can be friends."

She allowed a quick and perfunctory handshake. "Thank you." Equally as quickly, she withdrew her hand and her smile. Picard studied her, faced the fact he had no other choice but to withdraw, nodded and left. Beverly drew a deep breath. For a while, she had wondered whether her plain speech had offended him so deeply that he would not accept her as his chief medical officer. Apparently, everything Jack had said about him, and everything she had ever heard about him, was correct. He was hard, but fair. He accepted the fact he could be wrong and acknowledged it when he was. Maybe, just maybe, she would come to like him as much as Jack had. A vaguely disturbing thought drifted through her mind and was gone again in an instant.

Maybe she could come to like him *more.*

Riker's away team filed toward the transporter platform, quickly and efficiently checking their equipment as they moved. He had chosen Lieutenant Yar, Troi and Lieutenant Commander Data for individual strengths and traits, but also because they had worked well on the brief mission to the surface before the ship attack. He had justified the inclusion of Troi for her sensitivities to other life forms, sensitivities which they would undoubtedly need aboard the alien vessel. The android had also proven valuable in his ability to analyze information and present a conclusion—even if he was a little persistent in his queries about any references that were not literal facts.

"Set phasers on stun," Riker ordered. As the team quickly made the last check and settled on the transporter pads, he looked at the chief. "Ready."

The transporter chief rechecked his console carefully. "I'm locked on coordinates that should put you in the middle of that ship, sir, but our sensors can't get through whatever screens they have up. I don't know what I'm beaming you into, except it isn't their engines. *Those* we can read by the high intensity energy they put out."

Riker nodded. "Understood. Energize."

The transporter beam materialized them in what appeared to be a tunnel. Riker instantly recognized the symetrical shapes and unearthly soft glow. Data scanned his tricorder around, checking its readouts. "Most interesting, sir. Light, but no apparent light source. Construction of the walls—unknown. The tricorder cannot analyze it."

"It's the same construction as the tunnel under Farpoint Station," Tasha interjected.

Data looked up, quickly. "As I was about to comment," he said. Riker could have sworn the android sounded slightly miffed. "But you will notice, there is no sound of power or other ship sounds. No equipment."

"How does this ship run?"

Riker nodded to indicate a way down the tunnel. "Let's find out."

Tasha immediately took the point and led off in the direction he had signaled. Data kept up a constant tricorder scan of their surroundings, but shook his head at Riker to say the readings were useless.

Troi staggered, as if she'd been hit. Riker was at her side in two quick steps.

"Troi, what is it? Is it the same as you felt on the planet?"

"No, this is . . . different." She carefully lowered the mental shields she had snapped up when the empathic feeling had hit. A delicate probing analyzed it, and she looked up at Riker with a frown. "It feels much more powerful . . . full of *anger* . . . *hate.*

"Toward us?"

"No. It's directed down toward the old Bandi city."

Data moved forward eagerly. "Most intriguing again. The place that this vessel was firing upon wasn't the Farpoint Starbase but the home of those who constructed—" He abruptly stopped, glancing at Riker in something akin to embarrassment. "Sorry, sir. I seem to be commenting on everything."

Riker stifled a smile. "Don't stop. Your comments are valuable . . . and welcome."

They moved forward carefully, noting the sameness of the construction, the apparently endless tunnel. There were some branches off in other directions, but at Riker's instruction, Tasha kept bearing right.

"These corridors don't seem to lead anywhere— they just go on," Riker observed. "How do we get to other levels?"

"Speculation," Data said. "The aliens are able to pass through walls, perhaps through dimensions."

Tasha glanced at him with a frown. "Then why build walls at all?" she asked, always practical. Data nodded thoughtfully; she had made a nice point. Abruptly Riker's communicator sounded, and Picard's crisp voice crackled in transmission.

"Picard to Riker. Report."

"Riker here. This is turning out to be a very long tunnel or corridor that we've beamed into, sir. No ship's crew in sight; no sign of mechanisms or circuitry . . ."

"Keep reporting in, Commander. Picard out."

Riker glanced around at the others. "Our captain seems a little impatient."

"Oh, no sir," Data said brightly. "He just dislikes breaking in new officers."

"Thank you for telling me that, Data."

"You're welcome, sir."

Data would have gone on, at length, if Troi hadn't suddenly interrupted sharply. "*Groppler* Zorn, sir . . . in great fear." She pointed down the tunnel toward an intersection. "Just ahead." They hurried forward, Troi in the lead. She waved a hand at Riker to indicate something else. He stopped beside her as she paused to analyze it. "There's a different feeling to the corridor here, sir. *Very* different—"

Zorn's voice split the air, quivering with pain. "No, *please!* No more!"

The team ran around the curved wall of the intersection and skidded to a halt, staring ahead. Zorn was held suspended off the deck in the center of a cylindrical forcefield. They could see its edges glittering softly, outlining it. The forcefield sparkled, and they heard an ominous click. Zorn writhed and twitched, shrieking in pain.

"No! Please! No more! Please, no more!"

Riker and Tasha moved toward him and were brought up sharply by the leading edge of the forcefield. "Data. Check the extent of the forcefield." Data nodded, but he had begun scanning with his tricorder the moment they had seen the barrier. Zorn moaned in pain again, and Riker turned his attention to the unfortunate Bandi administrator. "Zorn. Can you hear me?"

Zorn slowly managed to lift his head and look toward them. Riker was shocked by the alien's pain-filled face, his features twisted into a grimace of intense agony. "Please. I can't talk to it. Make it stop the pain. Please . . ."

"Has the alien communicated—?" Troi broke off, spinning to face Riker as realization shot through her mind. "That's it, sir! It's just *one* alien I'm sensing here."

Zorn groaned again and twitched as something in the forcefield shot agony through his bones. *"Please!* I don't understand what it wants."

Troi glanced at Riker and shook her head. "Not true. He does know—and he's afraid."

Data completed his scan of the forcefield and moved to hold out the tricorder for Riker to see. "The forcefield is one meter in diameter, but it goes from ceiling to floor. I cannot pinpoint a source. But see this, sir—" He pointed to a specific reading on the tricorder, and Riker's eyebrows lifted in surprise. Riker pulled his phaser from its place and readjusted the setting.

"Heavy stun," he ordered. "Concentrate your fire on mine." He and Data raised the weapons and aimed directly at Zorn.

"No, no! Please don't!" Zorn screamed.

The phaser fire hit the forcefield, and a brilliantly colored glow spread over the entire face of it. Suddenly, it winked out, and Zorn's body flopped to the floor free of restraint. Tasha and Data ran forward to help him. Riker turned away to activate his communicator. "Riker to *Enterprise.*"

Troi felt the now-familiar touch of the alien mind in her own, and it troubled her. There was still the anger, but she sensed it was directed almost solely at Zorn. And there was questioning . . . Suddenly, Troi jerked alert. A strange, writhing tendril of plasma had extended itself from the wall and was swaying toward Riker. *Imzadi!* her mind screamed.

Other tendrils were reaching out from the walls toward Data and Tasha as they crouched over Zorn's body. Troi was grabbed from behind, a slim tentacle whipping around her waist and holding her in place. Riker was still calling into the communicator, "*Enterprise,* come in! Beam us—" Another tentacle slipped around his neck, beginning to throttle him.

On the *Enterprise,* Picard could hear the muffled sound of Riker's voice as it came over the communicator. He leaned toward his own communications panel anxiously and snapped, "Transporter Chief, yank them back! *Now!*"

Worf, manning the Ops station, suddenly turned to Picard, pointing at the viewscreen. "Captain!"

Picard glanced up and paused, staring at the amazing image now captured on the huge screen. The mighty vessel was beginning to *change,* its firm, hard edges seeming to melt into something softer, something unexplainable. "What in heaven . . . ?"

A blinding flash of light flooded the bridge, announcing *Q*'s return. This time, the alien wore the uniform of a Starfleet captain, complete to the four gold disks of rank. Picard glowered, resenting *Q*'s elevation to his own command level.

"Your time is up, Captain," *Q* intoned.

Picard ignored him and snapped into his command panel, "Transporter Chief, do you have their coordinates?" He waited a second, expecting the quick response. When it didn't come, he leaned forward anxiously. "Transporter Chief!"

Q casually stepped to the side of the command chair, smiling pleasantly. "He can't hear you, Captain."

Picard touched his own insignia communicator to activate it. "Transporter Chief, come in!" Dead air. *Q*'s smile widened. Picard turned to him angrily. "*Q,* I have people . . . in trouble over there . . . !"

Q lowered himself into the command chair, lazing in it with his booted feet outstretched. Picard held up a hand as other bridge personnel started forward angrily. "Everyone, at ease! That's an order." The others backed off, still angry, but obeying. Picard hated having to appeal to the alien, but he had to do something about the away team. "My people are in trouble, *Q*. Let me help them." He paused, took the final plunge. "I'll do whatever you say."

The alien gave him a strangely sweet smile and dropped his hand downward, his fingers flicking outward in a fan. Almost instantly, there was a peculiar sound that Picard could not identify. It was vaguely like a transporter beam, but not one of Starfleet's. An odd shimmering appeared in the air between the command chair and the forward stations. It resolved itself into five distinct shapes and, to Picard's relief, finally materialized as Riker, Data, Troi, Tasha, and Zorn—all whole and healthy.

"You'll do whatever I say?" *Q* asked smoothly.

Picard hesitated and finally nodded. He was a man of his word; he had given it. He wouldn't take it back, even if what the alien wanted was something Picard didn't want to give—and he had a feeling that would be exactly what *Q* wanted. "It seems I did make that bargain if you would return the team safely."

"The agreement isn't valid, then, sir," Troi said. "It wasn't *Q* who saved us."

Picard shot a glance at her, but *Q* was on his feet, interjecting quickly. "Save yourselves!" He pointed at the viewer. "It may attack you now."

The captain turned toward the main viewscreen and realized that the mystery vessel, in its changed form, was drifting closer to the *Enterprise*. "What is that thing?"

"That's what sent us back, Captain," Riker said.

"How do you know that?"

Troi moved forward again, earnestly. "I can feel it. It is not merely a vessel, sir. Somehow it is *alive.*"

"She lies!" *Q* shouted. "Destroy it while you can." He rushed toward Tasha, standing at the Weapons and Tactical Station. "Make phasers and photon torpedoes ready!"

"No! Do *nothing* he demands," Picard ordered. He turned to *Q* angrily. "You seem to have the idea that wearing that uniform gives you the right to give orders to my crew. It doesn't."

Zorn moved forward, weary and still weak from his painful ordeal. "But that thing was killing my people, Captain . . ."

"True, and the question is why? Was there a reason?"

Zorn lowered his eyes and shook his head. *Q* pushed in again, pressing Picard. "It is an unknown, Captain. Isn't that reason enough?"

"If you had earned that uniform, you'd know that the *unknown* is what brings us out here!" Picard snapped.

Q sniffed and turned away haughtily. "Wasted effort," he tossed off, "considering the level of your intelligence."

Picard sensed the alien backing off. He was not threatening or harrying now, not the bully boy. *Q* was reduced to throwing verbal barbs. In Picard's experience, that usually translated into a weakened position. "Let's test that," he said pleasantly. He turned to

Zorn. "Starting with the tunnels you have under Farpoint, *Groppler.*"

"Identical to the ones on that space vessel over there," Riker put in. "Why was it punishing you, Zorn? Perhaps in return for pain *you* caused some other life form?"

Picard pressed in on the Bandi administrator. Zorn flinched away from him, refusing to meet Picard's eyes. "We did nothing wrong!" he finally snapped. "The creature drifted down outside our city. It was weak . . . starving . . . it had been injured in space. We are not heartless. We tried to help it . . ."

"Thank you," Picard interrupted. "That was the missing part. Lieutenant Yar, rig main phaser banks to deliver an energy beam."

"Aye, sir." Tasha was puzzled as to Picard's intention; but her long slim fingers automatically went to the Weapons and Tactical Station console, calling for the powering up of the energy beam.

Picard looked back at Zorn. "You say you tried to help it. That wouldn't have made this creature so angry it's bent on wiping out every Bandi it can sense."

Zorn wriggled uncomfortably. The Bandi had needed the creature so much. It had done all they asked of it, even if it had needed some . . . coercion. "The creature requires energy to live, and we had it in abundance. It can read thought images. It could create anything we could think of . . . but we had to ration its energy to control it . . ."

Riker sighed. "It had to be conceivable that somewhere in the galaxy there could exist creatures able to convert energy into matter."

"And into specific patterns of matter, much as our transporters—and our holodecks—do," Data added.

Tasha had been watching the main viewscreen as she focused and refined the energy beam Picard ordered. Now she snapped, "On the viewer, Captain."

The vessel had begun to soften its edges further, melting into an amorphous lovely shape shot with soft, pulsing colors. "Zorn, you captured something like that, didn't you? And used it."

"It wanted to do it," Zorn protested. "To repay our kindness."

"You imprisoned it," Troi said harshly. "For your own ends."

"No, we just asked it to build something . . . large."

"It created Farpoint Station for you," Riker said. Then he corrected himself. "No . . . like that ship out there, it *is* Farpoint Station."

On the viewscreen, they could see the vessel creature flowing into a new shape. It extended feathery tendrils as it began to sink downward, toward the planet and the station below.

"Warn my people, please!" Zorn begged in panic. "They are in danger. Tell them to leave Farpoint Station immediately!"

Q thrust his way into the debate again. "He's lied to you, Captain. Shouldn't you let his people die?"

"Is that what you, in your advanced civilization, would recommend?" Picard inquired acidly. He didn't wait for a reply, but turned to Data at Ops. "Transmit this message to the Bandi. 'Leave Farpoint Station at once, for your own safety.' Continue transmission whether you get a response or not."

"Aye, sir." The android immediately began tabbing in the commands that would send the continuous message.

Troi had taken her seat at the left of the captain's chair and was staring at the viewscreen where the vessel creature still sank ominously toward the planet. "It was a pair of creatures I sensed. One down there in grief and pain and hunger, the other up here, filled with anger and hate . . ."

"And firing not on the new space station, but on the Bandi and their city."

Picard looked at Troi for confirmation of his next statement. "Attacking those who captured its . . . its mate?"

She swiftly examined the feelings and sensitivities she had received and shook her head. "Not quite the right word, sir." She slid a glance at Riker. "Perhaps the Betazoid word 'imzadi' comes closer."

The first officer blushed.

"Energy beam ready, sir," Tasha said.

"Lock it on Farpoint Station, Lieutenant Yar."

Q had begun to get annoyed at being ignored. Had these humans forgotten the bargain Picard had made? No one was doing what he wanted. They seemed to have decided he wasn't important. "I see now this was too simple a puzzle. But generosity has always been my weakness."

Picard continued to ignore *Q*. He nodded to Tasha. "Let it have whatever it can absorb. Energize."

Tasha tabbed a quick command into her console and glanced up at the main viewscreen. The huge screen's point of view shifted as Data operated his panel to follow the track of the thick, pale blue energy beam downward toward Farpoint Station. It struck the middle of the big station and seemed to be absorbed directly into it. Tasha watched her panel intently, caught a signal that brought her alert. "Now getting feedback on the beam, sir."

"Discontinue it," Picard said. *"Groppler* Zorn, there'll soon be no Farpoint Station if I'm right about this."

"A lucky guess!" *Q* shot in.

The others continued to ignore him. Zorn, who had no idea of who the alien was, took the others' lead and appealed directly to Picard. "Please believe me, Captain, we did not mean to harm the creature. It was starving for energy . . ."

"A need which you perverted for your own purposes."

"But we *did* feed it!" Zorn wailed, as if that small generosity absolved the crime. They *had* cared for the creature; if it had died, they would have been bereft. Of course, they might have cared more for the loss of the material possessions they would have lost than they would have for the death of the creature; but they would have mourned the loss.

"You fed it only enough to keep it alive, to force it to shape itself into the form you needed—"

"Sir," Data interjected. He nodded toward the viewscreen as Picard looked around.

Farpoint Station was shimmering, coalescing, growing soft around the edges. Slowly, it flowed into the shape of a gossamer creature, feathery light as it gracefully rose from its captivity. The vessel creature, larger, but equally beautiful, descended toward its mate.

"Sir," Troi breathed, "it's wonderful! A feeling of joy. And gratitude."

The bridge crew, Zorn and *Q* watched the screen as the two aliens closed, reaching toward each other with glowing, writhing extensions of delicate matter/energy. The tendrils touched and twined sinuously, and then both creatures began to move upward, past the *Enterprise* in orbit.

"Great joy and gratitude," Troi said quietly. "From both of them."

Q sniffed disdainfully as the gracefully moving aliens pushed further away from the planet, heading for the depths of space. "So dull, once you know the answers."

Picard whirled on him angrily. "Do you use other life forms for recreation?"

"If so, you've not provided the best."

"Leave us! We've passed your little test. We've danced to your tune, and we no longer enjoy the melody."

Q smiled appeasingly, holding out his hands in a gentling gesture. "Temper, temper, *mon capitaine . . .*"

It hadn't worked very well before. It didn't work now. *"Get off my ship!"* Pickard's roared.

At least *Q* had a sense of timing. He bowed toward Picard mockingly and chuckled. "I do so only because it suits me to leave. But I will not promise never to appear again." The blistering white flash of light carried him away, leaving the bridge complement alone with Zorn.

"Now, about Farpoint Station," Picard began.

The Bandi administrator seemed lost and forlorn, his face haggard with despair. He gestured toward the main viewscreen, which Data had brought to focus on what had been Farpoint Station. The Bandi city remained, damaged by the creature's attack. Beside it, the yellow desert winds of the planet stirred dust in the empty space where the station had once been. "There is no Farpoint Station, Captain. You will have to report to Starfleet that the Bandi have nothing to offer them."

Picard studied the screen for a moment, then he turned to Zorn thoughtfully. "You still have an ideal location for a station."

"Location, yes. Nothing more. We had hoped Farpoint would be our link to the outside worlds . . . a way for our people to flourish again. I see now. We chose . . . an *incorrect* way to accomplish it. To our detriment."

"Starfleet is still interested in Farpoint. With work and cooperation from you and with Federation assistance, this could still be a valuable staging planet for us. Are the Bandi willing to try?"

Zorn looked up, hope starting to erase the worry lines on his face. Truly, all they'd ever wanted was the opportunity to live on, to extend their racial heritage, and to grow by touching other cultures. "I think," he said slowly, "we would be very willing."

"Good," Picard said, smiling. "In that case, we have a great deal to discuss."

"I will be honored," Zorn said. He bowed humbly toward Picard, but the captain waved it away and gestured the administrator toward his command chair to confer with him.

Riker noticed Data running a program at Science Station 1 and moved up the ramp toward him. Data glanced around as the first officer joined him. "I was just taking a final reading on the creatures. I find it interesting that their conversion of energy into matter is so total that our instruments were unable to detect them as life forms when they were in that state."

"Very interesting, Commander—"

"Just Data, sir."

Riker smiled and went on. "Data. I wanted you to know I found your performance of duty absolutely faultless."

"My programming is of exceptionally high quality, sir," the android replied serenely.

"Yes. What I really mean is—I didn't find it as difficult as I thought to work with you."

"I could say the same, sir."

Riker persisted. "I'm trying to apologize if I said anything that offended you before."

Picard's mellow voice broke in quietly. "Well, Number One . . ."

"He must approve of you, sir," Data said softly. "Or he would not call you Number One."

Riker looked at Data and found the steady yellow eyes were oddly sincere. *I wonder how he manages that?* Riker thought. But the captain had summoned him, and he moved quickly down into the command well. "Yes, sir."

Picard had risen from his command chair to escort Zorn into his ready room. "It certainly has been an unusual welcome aboard. But there's still a lot to do before we can leave orbit." He noticed the bemused expression on Riker's face as the tall man slid into the first officer's chair. "Some problem, Commander?"

"Just hoping this isn't the usual way our missions will go, sir."

Picard screwed up his face in mock consideration and finally shook his head. "Oh, no, Number One. I'm sure most of them will be much more interesting."